SARGE AND THE
SAILOR BOY

First Edition

Published by The Nazca Plains Corporation
Las Vegas, Nevada
2009

ISBN: 978-1-935509-66-0

Published by

The Nazca Plains Corporation ®
4640 Paradise Rd, Suite 141
Las Vegas NV 89109-8000

PUBLISHER'S NOTE
Sarge and the Sailor Boy is a work of fiction created wholly by *Michael
Gleich's* imagination. All characters are fictional and any resemblance
to any persons living or deceased is purely by accident. No portion of
this book reflects any real person or events.

Cover Photos,
Esther Hildebrandt and Gansovsky Vladislav

Art Director, Blake Stephens

DEDICATION

To the boys and bars of San Francisco and the music of Janis Joplin that filled the airwaves of the city by the bay.

SARGE AND THE SAILOR BOY

First Edition

Michael Gleich

CHAPTER ONE

The square-jawed swabby looked in the mirror, moved his white sailor's hat forward just a bit, and then grinned at his reflection. His white bell-bottom pants fit snug across a perfect bubble-butt. And his shirt did the same with his pouted nipples pressed against the fabric. He knew he looked good. Sarge wouldn't want it any other way.

Tim was ready for shore leave, after six months at sea, and Sarge was ready too.

He knew where to report, and as Tim pulled back the bamboo curtain and walked into the seedy hotel run by Madam Woo, an old Chinese whore from Singapore, he knew he was in for a good time. Madam Woo provided what her customers liked: booze and privacy, she made sure they had plenty of both.

Tim walked past the rickety wood stairs that led to the cheap rented rooms of Madam Woo. He went to the bar where an old salt named Bull was the barkeep. Grizzled, with an anchor tattoo on one arm and a mermaid on the other, he had a short, chewed up stogie parked on the side of his mouth. He didn't take shit from anyone. If somebody got out of line, pulled a knife, or offended Madam Woo, which was hard to do, they were picked up and thrown on their ass on a wharf not fit to see in daylight. Bull didn't change his T-shirt very often. But nobody said anything to him about it—nobody.

Tim ordered whiskey.

"You're lucky he ain't here yet," Bull said, "You might have time for another one."

"Thanks Bull," he said as he pulled a bill out and put it on the bar.

When the bartender sat the drink down, Tim picked it up, studied it for just a second before he downed the drink in one gulp and sat the glass back for another. Bull was ready and poured it while Tim waited.

The second one was to linger over until he heard Sarge's boots. He knew the sound well and made sure his ear was tuned to pick up their drumbeat over the noise of the jukebox. The sailor glanced quickly around the room, to check out the clientele. Dock workers, construction men, marines, the bar wasn't for sissies. No fucking suits came to this bar for a cocktail.

Madam Woo hadn't changed a thing, she never did, except to extract cash from anybody who started a fight and tore up the place. The red silk lanterns that hung from the ceiling omitted just enough light to see. The walls were of paneled wood and the floor, solid oak with wooden tables and chairs, that creaked when sat on, were placed on the floorboards for the men to play cards, if a card game was on their minds. The long worn bar-top was made of wood from an old sailing ship. Names of sailors and their pleas were scarred on the well worn planks. When Madam Woo was there, she sat at the end of the bar. Her black silk dress with red-edged slits up the sides, hung on her small frame like the adornment on an ancient carved goddess. She would have a long cigarette holder held in one hand to smoke Egyptian cigarettes. Her nails were long too. And though she was old in years, she had her make-up on as if expecting the fleet. Near where she sat, a

2

cast-iron cauldron for incense was held up by three black dragons that snaked around its sides. Wisps of sandalwood smoke melded with the stink of men and what they did.

Sarge took Tim to Madam Woo's the first time he met him. She ran one of her long-curved fingernails over one of Tim's nipples that Sarge had played with while they stood at the bar drinking.

She crooned with glee and used her long fingernail to flick the swollen nub laid bare from Sarge pawing him on the way to the bar. "Wish my nipples stood out like that. What you do Sarge? Make his titties so nice."

"Shit Woo, this mother-fucker, he's so fuckin' horny. Them nips of his just cry to be sucked on." Sarge downed his whiskey and pulled Tim to his side. Taking the nipple in his mouth, he began to suck on it, playing his tongue over the swollen gland.

Tim remembered that day. He could still feel Sarge's teeth biting and chewing his tit. Sarge sucked on the plump nipple until Tim thought he would scream. Then, as Sarge flicked his tongue back and forth on the succulent nub, his hand slipped under the sailor's bell-bottoms and cupped the boy's butt-cheeks, his meaty fingers pushed on the hairless moist butt-hole. Sarge sucked on Tim's tit and fingered-fucked that bubble ass all the while Madam Woo smoked her cigarette. She seemed to enjoy hearing Tim moan and wreath like a Saigon whore.

Others watched too.

The longshoremen, tanked up on beer and whiskey, their grizzled faces grinned at Tim with his head lolling back in a state of ecstasy. The marines, playing poker, stopped for a few minutes to listen to Tim's groans of lust and they gazed at the sailor's crotch that bulged so that you could see the boned dick and the balls heavy in their sack.

The thirteen buttons pulled at its package, their threads stretched between them and the white cotton, damp with cock goo. They could see the sailor was cut, so rigid the veins in Tim's dick pressed against his navy whites in want that fateful day when he first met Sarge.

"If he was China girl, I make big money." Woo said in her matter-of-fact-way. She flicked the ash balanced on the long end of her cigarette holder.

"Well he ain't. He's one hundred percent Navy, just as I like them. Ain't ya Sailor Boy?"

Tim looked up at Sarge's coal black eyes and stared into their dark pools.

"Oh, Sarge. Yeah, I'm your mate alright. Jesus, Sarge, when you goin' to fuck me?"

"You're just beggin' for my dick ain't ya, Sailor Boy. You want that fuckin' horse cock in ya all the time, don't ya? I can feel how moist that tight hole is. Feel it suck on my fingers fucking your hot fuckin' little hole.

"Ah, fuck Sarge. I gotta have your dick soon. Can I suck it? Get it all slicked up so ya can fuck me. I'll let ya slam me Sarge. Bone me with that fuckin' dick of yours Sarge. Please? I just gotta have it."

"You'll get it sailor. You're gonna get all the fucking dick you ever wanted."

Sarge pulled his fingers out of Tim's tight ass and put them in the sailor's mouth.

"You get them slicked up sailor. You fuckin hear me? Slime those digits if you want them stuck up your ass."

Tim worked the fingers in his mouth. He wanted to impress Sarge how he could take anything he gave him. He wanted to be Sarge's fuck toy, to be used and abused.

He gurgled when Sarge shoved the thumb in and reached in the back of Tim's throat. He coughed up thick coats of slime as Sarge fucked Tim's throat with his hand.

The bar could see the sailor's neck swell out like a python swallowing prey. Sarge pulled out his slicked up hand and shoved it back in Tim's pants, back to that hot fucking puckered hole.

"Yeah sailor, we're gonna get you all ready. See those longshoremen? They been wantin' some of that ass of yours since you came in. Wanna give that tight little pucker of yours a workout? I bet you do, huh Sailor Boy."

Sarge shoved a few digits into Tim's ass and began to saw back and forth on the tight hole.

"Sarge, fuck me. Fuck me Sarge. Please I gotta have your dick."

Some of the longshoremen heard Sarge and walked over. Standing nearby they watched Sarge's fingers work under the cloth of Tim's pants as he finger fucked the young sailor.

Tim's eyes glazed over, he grunted with each thrust of Sarge's fingers. Tim went limp and laid his head against the sergeant's chest, lapping the nipple that poked out of the marine's opened khaki shirt.

The longshoremen gathered close and reached out to feel Tim's hot smooth body. They tweaked his nipples and whispered nasty things in his ears. What they wanted him to do. What he was going to do for them, and all the while the sailor groaned and begged for dick.

"It's time sailor to use that ass of yours. Strip ya fuckin' swabby."

Tim quickly came out of his daze, as he pulled his shirt off. The men popped the buttons on his pants and stripped him down. Sarge laid him over two bar stools. His ass perched up at one end, ready for the dock workers, with his head in the crotch of the sergeant. The marine sat on his stool and lit a cigar. As he held the match to the stogie, he watched Tim mouth the mound of hot dick in his pants.

Once the cigar's end glowed red and the thick gray-blue smoke filled his nostrils he reached over and spread the ass cheeks of the sailor.

"Plug him boys. Fuck the hell out of that prime navy ass."

The bubbled butt gleamed with spit and sweat. Its tight hairless hole puckered and gapped waiting for cock.

A big Jamaican with a smooth ebony head and thick gold earrings came up behind Tim and pulled out a black boa of a cock. It hung to his knees and swung side to side as the Jamaican walked. He grabbed it by his two hands and began to shove it in the tight white ass.

"Mon, this white meat sure is good." He said and slapped Tim's butt.

The sailor could feel inch after inch of dark meat go up his hole. He thought the Jamaican had a python for a cock, and still more went in his butt. Just as Tim started to sweat, he felt course black pubes grind against his hairless white ass.

Sarge let go of the tight ass cheeks and watched them mound over the dick going in and out of the stretched out hole. He grabbed the sailor by his blond hair and raised his head up.

"You like that fucker? You like that Jamaican reaming out your pretty little hole?"

Tim could only grin from ear to ear. His blue eyes opened and blinked once then twice when the stud fucking him slammed him good. It made Tim belch.

"You need cock boy. You need fuckin' dick down your cock-sucking throat. Don't ya sailor?"

Tim went to speak but before he found the words to answer, Sarge pulled his slab of cock-meat out and shoved it in the sailor's mouth.

Sarge chewed his cigar, and with both hands holding onto Tim's curly blond locks, pumped the sailor's face with his dick.

"You're getting' fuck good now aren't ya Sailor Boy. Huh, answer me you little fuck."

All Tim could do was to gurgle around the cock lodged deep in his throat but Sarge could see his head move up and down, trying to answer his question and slapped the sailor's cheeks, first the right and then the left cheek.

"Gotta loosen that pussy mouth of yours sailor, gotta get you all loosy-goosey for a good fuckin'."

Sarge pulled the cigar out of his mouth and motioned for Bull to pour him another drink. While he watched Tim work his mouth up and down on his cock, he smoked his cigar and drank his whiskey.

The Jamaican ground his crotch into the white bubble-butt cheeks of the sailor and shot a wad that oozed around his fuck stick. Finished, he pulled the cock out and sat down on a bar stool nearby.

A big burly Pole was next. His dick already hard and as thick as a fire plug, he pushed it into the slicked up hole of the sailor's. The Pole's hand could wrap around less than half of the cock he fed to the sailor's hungry hole.

"Tight. Yah, good and tight." The Pole grabbed Tim's hips and pulled them back while he shoved his cock in.

Sarge looked to see Tim's butt-hole spread tight around the extra wide cock. When the Polak pulled part way out, Tim's ass-lips held on to the fat dick like a rubber glove.

The dockworker's plaid shirt was opened, the black hairs on his massive chest and gut glistened with sweat and when he shoved his fucking dick back in the hot hole and Tim's guts went back as well. Sweat from the Pole sprayed the sailor's back.

"He's good fuck. Yah, sure is good pussy you got there Sarge. Tight"

"Shit Johann, I hope that fuckin' pussy ripper of yours don't stretch him out too much."

Sarge watched the girth of the hard as steel cock plummet the tight little ass of the sailor. The navy man's butt cheeks spread wide to take the girth of the Pole's plunger and the bubble cheeks jiggled when he reamed the sailor deep.

The Pole didn't last long and when he came nothing could seep out of the tight fit, instead, Tim's gut swelled as the longshoreman pumped cock juice into the boy's gut.

"Das gut. You like sailor? You like Polish sausage up your tight hole?"

Tim could hardly wiggle with his mouth and throat full of Sarge's dick and the ramrod stuck up his ass that had him plugged as if he had sat on a fire hydrant.

When Johann pulled his meat out there was a suction noise, and Tim's butt-hole spewed out gobs of jizz that dripped to the floor.

Before the next dock worker took over, Sarge stood up and told the guy to fuck Tim's throat. He was going to fuck Tim next before he was stretched all to hell.

Sarge walked in back of Tim and shoved his cock up the hot hole. The sailor's butt snapped back in shape as if it was made of elastic and Sarge grew a smile.

"This here, fucker has an ass made to be fucked. Damn if he ain't just as tight as the day I took his cherry."

Sarge slapped the butt cheek of the sailor and said, "You're prime mother-fuckin-navy ass. You know that sailor? You know what a hot fuck you are?"

Before Tim could answer, a big stud with a crew-cut shoved his cock in Tim's mouth and began to screw his face.

The face fucker lifted his tight white T-shirt and exposed his six-pack abs, his small waist whipped back and forth as he fucked Tim's mouth and the shore man's hand went up to play with one of his hard nipples.

"Matt you fucker. You got the prettiest titties." Sarge said.

"Fuck you Sarge. I sure like this sailor's mouth. Damn if he don't suck like a Hoover."

"He is good, that's a fact. You're lucky I'm in a good mood and don't mind sharing." Sarge slapped Tim's ass hard and made the sailor grunt.

"Mighty nice of you Sarge. Real good of you to be so generous with this here fuck of yours."

"That's better. Fuck his face good. He's been whining for some time now and needs a good fuckin' to settle him down."

"Happy to oblige," and with that, Matt started to piston fuck the sailor's gulping mouth. Tim's cheeks would bulge out with dick, and when Matt pulled back, Tim's cheeks sunk in showing he kept good suction on the prick screwing his mouth.

The sailor was in heaven. He had a hot guy with a hot dick fucking his throat and Sarge ramming his butt. Tim relaxed and let the men have their way with his holes. He felt Sarge's cock glide in and out, reaming him good. His butt-hole clasped Sarge and held on to his dick like a velvet glove. His tongue rubbed along the sheath of Matt's cock, tickling the end of the dick's head when he pulled out of his cock-sucking throat. He could do this all day, he thought, feeling the piston cocks working his holes, fucking him good.

Tim's dick, hard as a brick, slapped at the bar stool beneath him. Sarge was slamming his back door and reached under to milk Tim's fuck stick. He felt his cock gush as the jizz coated his belly and the stool. Matt tweaked his tit and started to shake, splattering Tim's tonsils with cock glue. Sarge slapped one ass cheek and then the other as he drove home in Tim's bubble butt. The whole crowd stopped to watch the triple orgasm take place, and listen to the men fuck.

Sarge smacked the sailor's butt one more time and said, "Yeah sailor take that dick. Take my fuckin' dick Sailor Boy." Then he shot his load deep in Tim's gut.

"Suck it. Yeah, suck my cock sailor. That's a boy. Suck my seed out, you fuckin dick-licker." Matt shot and watched Tim's throat milk the spooge from his dick.

The two men pulled out and smiled at each other while Tim lay between them panting like a dog in heat. Cum flowed from his ass and the side of his mouth as he lay over the two bar stools not wanting it to stop. His cock already hardened for another fuck.

CHAPTER TWO

There was a slight creak from the stairs that woke Tim from his memory of that first time with Sarge. He looked up to see Madame Woo glide down the stairs with her cigarette holder in hand, the smoke from its tip trailing behind her.

She walked over to her seat by the door and lit an incense stick, placing it in the iron cauldron. Then she sat down and looked over at Tim.

"So, Sailor Boy, you back for more? You waiting for Sarge?"

"Sure am Madame Woo. He should be here soon." Tim was still flushed from day-dreaming about the last time he was at Madame Woo's.

The old Asian woman tapped her cigarette holder and watched the ash on the end fall to the floor. "How come you so wiggly? You sitting on something Sailor Boy?"

"Oh Madame Woo, Sarge gave me something the last time we was together and I stuffed it in to surprise him."

"I don't think Sarge be surprised, Sailor Boy. Sarge expects you to wear it, doesn't he?"

"Madame Woo, you're embarrassing me. I'm just a farm boy from Nebraska."

Madame Woo took a long drag on the end of her ivory cigarette holder and made smoke rings when she exhaled.

"You were a farm boy, but now you sailor and you've fucked more men than all the cows in Nebraska. Isn't that right Sailor Boy?

Tim's cheeks turned rosy red and his blue eyes fluttered. "Shucks ma'am, guess I have, if you say so."

"What you say Bull?" asked Madame Woo.

"He's the best piece of ass on this here wharf. Like I said to Sarge last time they was here, 'Does Tim follow the fleet or does the fleet follow Tim?'"

The men laughed that sat around the bar while Tim sat squirming on his stool, blushing.

Madame Woo sucked at the cigarette holder, lifted her head and blew a smoke ring that circled one of the red silk lanterns that hung from the ceiling. She turned to Bull and tapped the end of the holder letting the ash fall to the floor.

"Bull? Where did you put Suit?"

Bull was wiping whiskey glasses and stopped for a moment to yell, "Suit. Front and Center."

From the bathroom came a young man dressed in a high fashion suit and polished shoes. His face had dirt and grime streaked on the cheeks and forehead, and his hands held what looked like socks he used for scrubbing.

Suit ran to the bar and stood at attention right in front of Bull.

"Sir. Yes sir!"

"Is the shitter cleaned, ass-wipe?"

"Sir, yes sir."

"It better be shithead. Madame Woo wants ya."

"Sir. Yes Sir."

Suit turned to Woo and then he saw that there were ashes near where she sat. He jumped down near her feet and licked the ash off the floor.

Madame Woo asked Bull, "Make sure bar is stocked and ready. With Sarge and Sailor Boy here, we'll be plenty busy."

"Suit!"

Suit got up off the floor and stood at attention in front of Bull.

"Sir. Yes Sir."

"Get the bar primed and ready for action, maggot."

"Sir. Yes Sir." Suit said and scurried behind the bar, checking on what was needed.

"I think I hear Sarge," Madame Woo said.

The bar's door open and Sarge's boots hit the deck.

"Sarge!"

Tim's grin was almost as fast as his feet in their haste to get the sailor next to the large man. Sarge took the cigar from his lips and held it while he tongue fucked the sailor's mouth. Tim cooed and pressed against the sergeant. The sailor's hand felt Sarge's bicep, his fingertips lingered where the bulged and tattooed muscle popped out like a cannon ball. Tim rubbed his groin on the marine's leg as if he was a dog, desperate to bone.

"Settle down sailor," Sarge said putting his cigar back in his mouth. "You'll get dick and plenty of it. Right boys?" he looked around at the other marines and longshoremen in the bar.

"Yeah!" was their response.

"You've been a good sailor? Huh, you haven't fucked half the ship while you were at sea did you?

"Oh, Sarge, I wouldn't unless you wanted me to."

"Well, I thought maybe you'd forget about Sarge once you boarded ship."

Sarge looked at Madame Woo and winked.

"Oh, Sarge how could I forget? It was the best time of my life!"

Tim remembered that first day when Sarge brought him down from their room upstairs after hours of being fucked and used by Sarge. Escorted naked, wearing only his sailor cap with Sarge's belt strapped around Tim's neck as a leash. He was spread out on a table so the men could double fuck his ass and shove their spent cocks in his throat for a good cleaning before going back to that hot hairless butt-hole. The boy's flopping dick spurted cock-snot over the men surrounding the table that mauled his tits, and pulled on his balls. They slapped the navy man's spurting cock every time it gooed.

"Bull." Sarge looked over at the bartender cleaning glasses. "Whiskey."

Bull came over with two shot glasses and an opened bottle of booze. He poured the shots and sat the bottle down between the glasses. Sarge handed Tim one of the shots and slapped his glass against it. The two men drank their shots quick and Sarge filled them up again. This time, as he held his cigar clamped in his teeth, he watched the sailor drink the shot while he reached behind him and felt for the butt-plug.

"You wearin' my present. Ain't you the sweet thing," he purred to the sailor.

"Oh, Sarge I gotta wear it. If I don't my damn asshole is so loose it sucks up my shorts."

Sarge grinned and put his hand inside the sailor's pants so he could pull on the butt-plug. "Now ain't that too bad. I thought my fist, jacking my cock off in your ass, might have loosened you up some. Well, guess you'll just have to get use to wearing it. Huh, Sailor Boy?"

"Oh I love it Sarge. It makes me feel like you're fucking me all the time, but it ain't you. It's just ten pounds of rubber cock."

"Nice to have the real thing. Ain't it fuck boy."

"It sure is Sarge."

"Finish your drink, and maybe I'll let you suck me some while I finish mine."

The sailor downed his drink and looked up at the sergeant's face, like a puppy dog wanting a bone. Sarge sipped on the lip of the glass and pulled on his own dick still in his khakis. His cock grew heavy inside its jock. The veined prick bulged at the crotch in an obscene way and the boy began to whimper.

"Please Sarge. Please let me suck it," he moaned while looking at the huge bulge and then up at the sergeant.

Salvia dripped from his mouth, the sailor's tongue licked at his lips and stuck his tongue out to show Sarge how he would lick the baby maker. "Ah, please Sarge. Let me taste it."

Sarge looked down at the sailor's imploring eyes.

"Well. I'll let you sniff it."

The sailor dove to his knees, his face grazed Sarge's pants taking in deep whiffs of the heady odors of jock sweat just under the khakis.

"Don't you fucking slobber on my pants dip-shit."

Tim licked at the drool that ran from his mouth. "I won't Sarge. Promise."

"You fuckin' better not." Sarge pushed his hips out, smashing his bulge in the sailor's face.

Tim made sure he didn't leave any drool, but he did sniff in the heady aroma of the sweat stained jock. Sarge watched him breathe in the aromas of his groin as he sipped his drink.

"Okay, Sailor Boy. Take that barracuda out."

"Oh, thank you Sarge. Thank you."

Tim reached to pull on the zipper, his eyes glazed. He stared at the soldiers bulge as if it was a pot of gold. A finger held the pull on the zipper and he listened to every click as he slowly and carefully pulled it over the mound. Tim's hands began to shake with anticipation, and when the heady aroma of jock sweat smacked his nostrils, he almost swooned. He sucked in the odor of the gods and his eyes lingered at how the pouch strained under its load.

It was hard for him not to stop then and feel the stained fabric, feel the flesh of the cock it held. He could see the head that waited for his mouth and tongue, the shaft yearning to break free to lodge in his throat.

Tim whimpered. The zipper became stuck on one the fibers of the jock. Now he would be delayed in having his prize, he almost cried at the thought and carefully backed up the pull before starting to tug it downward once again.

The work was delicate, the jock strained and used, pushed hard against the khaki pants so that Tim had to pull very carefully with no room left for error.

Sarge looked down at Tim. He chuckled to see how carefully the sailor took to his task. Tim's face was so close he could almost taste the jock. The prick and bag of balls encased inside, pushed at the mesh pouch and seemed to seek Tim's hot moist mouth. The sailor's lips, almost grazed the pouch, the sailor's tender lips puckered and could feel the heat from the pouch, as if it was a furnace of desire. His nostrils inhaled the aromas of Sarge, his sweat, piss and the pent up cum that waited for him to suck out.

The zipper was now pulled over the mound and near the end of it travel. The jock pouch heaved out, free to stretch to its limits. The weight of it hid Tim's administrative fingers. The jock pouch slapped against his lips and he couldn't help but swipe at the prize with his tongue.

"Sailor!"

Tim looked up at Sarge, the cigar chomped at the side of his mouth. His dark eyes sparkling back at him. The sailor's lips quivered in anticipation of tasting the hefty jock filled bundle.

The marines stopped their poker game. They too wanted to see the enormous cock spring to life. The longshoremen silenced their muttering to gander at the sailor opening the fly and the jock that made Tim's eyes cross.

Drool dripped off the tongue of the sailor, it fell in strings down on the floor between where his kneeling legs were spread.

"Did I tell you to lick my jock?"

"No sir, it just kinda hit my tongue when it flopped out of your khakis"

"It kinda hit your tongue." Sarge stepped up on his toes and then back down making the jock pouch jiggle right in front of the Sailor's face. "I might give this to someone else, someone that can do what I tell them. You want this jock, sailor? Do you want to taste it, feel it? Do you want to hold it and see how heavy my fuckin' cock and balls are sailor?"

"Yes Sir, I'm sorry sir. I'll be more careful sir."

"You better be Sailor Boy. You damn well better follow my orders. Do you hear me?"

"Sir. Yes sir."

"What did you say?"

"Sir! Yes sir!"

"That's better sailor. You want dick? You gotta earn it first."

"Sir! Yes sir!"

Sarge smiled and patted the top of Tim's curly blond hair as if he was a good dog waiting for his bone.

"You got that fly down yet Sailor?"

"Just a half of inch more Sarge."

Tim gently pulled the zipper the rest of the way down. It was hard to control his shaking hand, being so close to the pouch.

The sailor knelt there in front of Sarge, and stared at the jock pouch, mesmerized by it. Sarge puffed on his cigar, then laid it in an ashtray nearby. He picked up his drink and swallowed the amber colored whiskey. All the while he watched Tim's pretty blue eyes stare at his crotch. Drool from the sailor's mouth hung at the corner of his lips and the blond swabby's tongue would gently graze along his smile in anticipation of Sarge's order to service that jock and the cock and balls inside.

"What are you looking at sailor? You looking for dick? Is that it sailor? You want some cock in your mouth? You want to taste my fuckin' dick? Is that it sailor?

"Sir, yes sir, I would love to suck your cock. Please Sarge. Let me have it. Please, I'll suck you real good Sarge, I promise."

"Well, I'll let you sniff the jock, maybe even lick it. You want to sniff my fucking jock? Lick the pouch? It's raunchy as all hell, sailor. You wanna do that?"

Sarge took both hands and cupped the package to rub the jock's pouch over Tim's face.

"Oh, Sarge, I gotta have some dick. Please Sarge, let me suck on that jock of yours. Please Sarge."

His nose ran over the heady aroma of hot cock encased in the filthy jock. The yellow encrusted stains streaked the fabric and the outline of the great prick filled his view. He wanted to mouth the head. Lick the balls through the jock pouch. Savor the stringent flavor of cock-meat kept warm and moist.

"Go for it fucker," Sarge said as he reached for the whiskey bottle and poured himself another shot. As the sailor's tongue lapped over the outline of the cock's head, Sarge poured a little whiskey on the jock for his Sailor Boy.

The marines couldn't believe the profile of the sailor and the Sarge. They wondered how that fucking jock could fit in the sergeant's pants. It stuck out as big as the sailor's head as they watched the boy's tongue work the fabric of the jock. Pulling it with each swipe, pushing his mouth as far as he could into the pouch, the sailor's tongue never stopped covering every bit of encrusted, sweat-stained marine jock, filled with the most incredible cock and bag of marine balls.

"That's real nice, you clean that jock up Sailor Boy, clean it good. Maybe I'll let you have it for a hammock," Sarge laughed and scratched under his arm.

"Maybe when you're through licking that jock, I'll let you lick my pits. That be a treat for you sailor. Wouldn't it boy?"

Tim's mouth was so busy on the jock his words came out muffled. "Hmm, thaf be good, hmm."

"What the fuck did you say sailor. Do you want to sniff and lick my fuckin rank pits?"

The sailor quickly looked up and answered, "Sir! Yes Sir!"

"That's better sailor. Don't talk with your mouth full swabby, it ain't polite."

Tim looked up imploringly at Sarge, his blue eyes watering from the jock pouch he had stuffed in his mouth, yet he managed to nod his head in agreement and kept sucking on the pouch with that dick inside.

Sarge picked up his cigar again and puffed on it a few times before he took another swig of whiskey. He towered over Tim administering to the sergeant's jock pouch as if he was trying to swallow its cantaloupe size. The men in the bar found it hard to play cards. Their hands kept rubbing at their crotches and orders for whiskey went out to Bull, who had Suit running back and forth filling their glasses with a good kick in the ass to send him on his way.

"Now you take that fucker of mine out and suck on the head."

Tim couldn't believe what he heard and looked up at Sarge. It usually takes much longer before he can suck the head. He missed cleaning the boots and smelling the stink under Sarge's arms. He missed begging and pleading for just a taste of the mammoth dick.

"Oh, Sarge you're so good to me. Thank you. Thank you. Thank you." Tim pulled at the jock with his teeth. He crossed his eyes watching the great prick become exposed as he pulled the jock down.

His nose rubbed along the length, and he kept pulling until the damn thing sprung free and hung half way down Sarge's leg. Tim's tongue flicked at the leaking piss slit. He lapped at the groove on the head of the cock for anything it might offer. He nursed on it while both hands held Sarge's fucker up to his face.

Tim's tongue lapped at the head. He suckled at the piss slit every time it began to glisten with cock-goo. His tongue wound its way around the velvety organ, he kissed and licked, worshipping the cock-god and relished its manly scent and feel. The sailor's own prick was rigid and cried for release. The tight, little pucker of his ass began to suck on the butt-plug embedded in his ass. His hole clamped on the hefty butt-toy and tried to suck its flanged end up into his ass. The hairless pouted ass-lips quivered in their need to spread open for dick.

With all of Tim's work on the head of Sarge's dick, it began to glisten with his spit. Sarge poured another shot and downed it. He watched as his dick hardened into a battering ram of hot muscled cock. It stood rigid and boned out from his loins, covering the face of Tim who worshiped the cock and all the goodness that came from it.

"That's enough sailor. I need to nut. Now."

With that, Sarge grabbed the sailor by the scruff of his neck, picked him up, and bent him over the bar's top. Tim looked wild-eyed at Bull who's smirking face told him he was going to enjoy what Sarge was about to do. With one hand Sarge held the sailor against the bar. His other hand grabbed the sailor's pants and pulled them down. The sergeant then grabbed the butt-plug and pulled it with a yank. Tim's guts followed along and his ass lips grabbed at the last of the plug before they folded back into his hole. Sarge then slammed the butt-plug right in front of the sailor's face. It was coated with butt juice and slime and Tim could feel the heat that radiated from the plug being in his ass so long.

"Bull, hand me that old jock strap you have behind the bar. The one you use to hit the barflies with."

Bull pulled out a filthy old jock, crusted and damp. He handed it to Sarge who put the pouch over the cone of the butt-plug.

"Now you have something to lick while I fuck your ass."

With that, Sarge slammed his cock all the way in Tim's ass. The sailor's eyes bulged out and his face became red, he grunted and grabbed the side of the bar to hold on as Sarge slammed him.

While fucking Tim's plump little ass, Sarge poured some whiskey on the jock covered butt-plug.

"Start slurping while it's hot, boy. You don't want dinner to get cold. Do you?" He punctuated the last word by grinding his baby-maker deep in the sailor's ass.

Tim's tongue reached out and began to slurp on the plug, licking the pouch smeared with whiskey, butt juice, and slime. Each slam from Sarge pushed his mouth on the plug. The marines, sitting at the table, had stopped their card game again. The dockworkers put down their beers to watch Sarge's bull balls swing back and forth as he rutted the sailor. Sarge pile-drove Tim's ass with his hefty cock and as Tim groaned with each slam into his bubble butt, the sailor's tongue flicked out to lick the whiskey-covered jock mounted on the butt-plug.

A good twelve inches of cock would pull out from the sailor's ass-hole, leaving the head still firmly planted in Tim's butt. Then, in one long thrust, the cock was rammed back in the moist, hot hole. Sarge's nut-sack swung back and forth. They'd swing back and slap the marine's ass with a smack, and then swing forward, slamming the sailor's cock and balls.

"What a good fuck you are Sailor. Hot fuckin' ass. Yeah, I'm gonna cream in that fuck chute of yours Sailor Boy. I'm going to slam this baby-maker in your hot fuckin' hole and blast your fucking head off."

Tim held on to the sides of the bar and slurped the butt-plug and the cum-encrusted jock that covered it.

He kept his bubble-butt ass up in the air so Sarge could plunge his fuck-stick in deep and ream him good.

"Fuck me good Sarge. Fuck my ass real good."

The drill sergeant slammed those bouncy ass cheeks of Tim's that quivered and shook as they were fucked. Sarge smacked both of Tim's hard little butt cheeks.

"I'll fuck you sailor. I'll fuck you into the next Thursday, you fucking, cock-sucking bitch. Yeah, take my fuckin' dick. Take it."

Sarge slammed the little white butt. He pounded Tim hard on the bar top. The sailor's eyes bulged and he could feel the baby batter splat deep in his gut.

"Yeah, Sarge fuck me. Fuck me."

Sarge pulled Tim's head back by his blond curly hair and drove his tongue deep in Tim's mouth. The sailor raised his ass higher, like a cat in heat and squirmed on the fuck-stick inside his hot ass. Sarge felt Tim's throat as he tongue fucked the sailor's mouth.

CHAPTER THREE

The marine pulled off the sailor's mouth and whispered in his ear. "I'm gonna fuck that throat next. Fuck your god-damn throat like it was pussy."

You want Sarge to fuck your mouth, cock-sucker? You want that prick of mine deep in your throat sailor?"

Before Tim could answer, Sarge pushed his tongue back in the hot mouth of the navy man.

Tim played with the drill sergeant's tongue, he sucked in all the spit he could. He tried to swallow Sarge's tongue, treated it like a cock, a dick for him to worship, to love and fuck him with.

Sarge pulled out of the tight bubbled ass with a plop. His dick hung down and swung between his legs, dripping cock-goo from the piss slit. The sailor's pucker gaped open for a few seconds before the little rosebud snapped back, nice and tight as if it just passed a grape seed.

"Get down there boy and clean that fuckin' dick of mine and I'll plug ya again. Maybe."

"Sure Sarge."

Tim went to his knees, his boner sticking up between his spread legs and as he held on to Sarge's pants, he began to lap at the cock's shaft and head.

"Yeah, clean that prick good, sailor."

Tim held the hose like prick in both hands moving the cock around so that he could lick everywhere. His tongue slurped the head, worked its way into the ridges and veins of the cock. He licked up one side and down the other until he had the dick completely cleaned.

Sarge stood there with his stogie in his mouth and a drink in hand while he watched the sailor worship his cock.

"Don't forget the balls sailor."

"No sir. I won't sir."

With that, Tim snuggled his face under the heavy cock, his tongue reached out and lapped at the sack that hung large and pendulous from the sergeant's groin. He felt the heat from Sarge rutting his tight butt and the ball sack churning up more cock juice for him. The sailor could smell the acrid aroma of sweat, piss and man stink. The heady aroma intoxicated him and invigorated his lust.

Tim's voice came out from under Sarge's cock, muffled by the balls he worshipped. "Oh, Sarge I'm so fuckin hot Sarge. Your balls smell so fuckin' good."

"I bet they do Sailor. You better clean them good, they've been in that jock pouch for a while now."

Tim could smell the forced marches Sarge delighted in. The pushups he commanded and did with the troops. He whiffed the orders he gave to men who did everything the marine drill instructor told them to do.

Tim's tongue went to work. The slick muscle started at the base of the ball sack, where the sweat was encrusted on the hairs that caught every drop. He licked deep in the crevices to remove every salty bit with his tongue. His mouth lapped at the sides of the balls that hung out of the sergeant's fly. He hoped that he would be allowed to clean Sarge more thorough when the marine took his pants off. He wanted to get to the sergeants ass and deep into the crack. As it was, he tried his best to stretch his tongue, pushing it into Sarge's groin and taste what he could of where Sarge nut-sack attached deep between his legs. Tim's nostrils breathed in deep the heady aromas held in that dark area, the smells of marine khakis and jock. The moist odors of cock and balls held captive in a jock for days on end.

Finally, Tim had to come up for air, he had to force himself to take a breath before diving back in and rutting around Sarge's nuts.

His tongue coated with the delicious taste of man-sweat, he dove back down and gulped down one of Sarge's balls in his mouth. It filled his cheeks with his tongue pressed against it, feeling its hard egg shape before it plopped out and he sucked up the other to do the same.

Then Tim tried the impossible, he wanted to feel both of them in his mouth, and he tried, as best as he could, to slip his mouth around the other ball. He whimpered and whined with his struggle to get the ball in, struggled to have both balls in his mouth.

In his desperation, the sailor grabbed the corners of his lips with his fingers and stretched them until they hurt. He thought they might tear while he opened his jaws as wide as possible.

Sarge could feel what Tim was doing and looked down with a smile. He decided to help him out. With one hand he held the nut-sack, pushing his balls down tight and encouraged the sailor to take them.

"Come on fucker, you can do it. Suck those baby makers in. Suck up sailor. I want to see what your mouth looks like when you have both balls in there. Come on sailor, you can do it."

Tim struggled. He thought his jaw would unhinge, that it would break for sure and that his lips would rip to the cheeks if he spread them anymore. With a grunt and sheer grit the ball plopped in with the other. Tim's cheeks were filled up more than a squirrel's. Filled with the Sarge's hot ball-sack. His tongue lay flattened unable to move. The sailor had to breath through his nose, there was no room for anything but the nut-sack and he was in heaven.

"That'a boy sailor. Look fellas at the new trick Sailor Boy learned just now."

Sarge proudly displayed Tim hanging from his nuts. The sailor cheeks grotesquely stretched around the balls with his head hanging between Sarge's legs.

"Hey fellas, looks like I caught myself a nice size fish."

One of the longshoremen said, "Looks like a groper."

Someone else yelled out, "Naw, a large mouth bitch."

Madame Woo cackled on her chair, exhaled a smoke ring and asked, "Sarge, how you going to take the hook out?"

Sarge grabbed his dick and slapped it against Tim's face, with the puffed out cheeks and his blue eyes, wild eye, looking at the crowd as Sarge paraded him around. "I'll just bitch slap him with this here barracuda until he falls off."

The crowd roared after that while Tim was dragged along the floor, his mouth firmly engulfed on Sarge's fat balls.

Sarge dragged Tim over to an empty table and with the help of two other marines, placed Tim on top of the table. Sarge straddled the sailors head and Tim's eyes stared up at the hard muscled butt of the drill instructor.

Some of the men began to gather around the table. They reached out and pinched the sailor's rubbery nips that looked like tiny cocks. They played with his prick, slapping it back and forth and watched it trail cock-goo from the piss slit like a spider building a web.

Sarge held Tim's throat with one hand, and with the other, pulled his balls out of the sailor's mouth. It made the sound of a cork popping off a bottle of champagne and the sailor had only enough time for a quick gasp of air before Sarge's cockhead was stuffed into the sailor's mouth.

"Can we fuck him Sarge?"

"Yeah sure, why not. Lift his legs up to me. Will ya?

"Sure Sarge."

A marine grabbed Tim's legs, his pants bunched up around his ankles and shoved them back to Sarge.

The drill sergeant pulled the head of his cock out, then he took hold of the pants, pushed the sailor's legs all the way back and fitted Tim's pants behind his head. Then Sarge unfastened his belt and dropped his pants before he shoved his cock back in the sailor's mouth.

Tim's ass was spread wide open. His pants held his legs to each side of his head and now he was looking up at the hairy muscled butt of Sarge's ass crack. Sarge's balls fell over Tim's nose and his mouth was stuffed with Sarge's big cock.

Tim's prick lay against his belly and gooed cock-snot that one of the marines used to lube up the sailor's asshole. Then he scooped up more and smeared his own dick and shoved it in the sailor's hot, tight ass.

"Damn this fucker has a hot fucking hole. I guess all that friction from you fucking him Sarge made it hot as a hundred dollar whore."

Sarge was fucking the sailor's throat and mouth, pulling his cock out to the head before he shoved it back in and watched how Tim's throat swelled as the thick ramrod engorged the sailor's throat.

"He's just one hot fuck. His throat is hot, his ass is hot. I think he has a furnace in there that makes him so hot."

"Better than any pussy. I can tell you that." The man said fucking the sailor in the ass.

"That's because he's a hundred percent Navy. That's a fact. He's just one hot fuckin' Sailor Boy."

Tim's eyes looked happy and why shouldn't they. Sarge was proud of him. He was the best damn fuck in the Navy and he had his mouth full of hot Sarge cock and his ass was pumped by another big dick marine. He looked up at Sarge's hard hairy ass and watch it work back and forth fucking his mouth with one of the biggest dicks around. He tried to get closer to Sarge's crack. Tried to raise his head a little and sniff when that big, hard, hairy butt-crack came close to his nose. But he could only get so close.

Just close enough to get a whiff of all the man scents inches from his nose. Sarge's thick dick hammered at Tim's mouth. The sailor's lips, stretched by Sarge's ball sack, were rubbery and flexible, they moved along the cock as it pumped in and out of his mouth. Then the mammoth cock was shoved down Tim's throat and his lips were pushed back, his cheeks filled with Sarge's entire dick.

The marine fucking Tim's ass shot his load. He walked to Tim's side to wipe his dick off on the sailor's tits. The longshoreman that was slapping Tim's cock and balls now walked between the sailor's legs and slammed his salami in the hot ass. It didn't take long for him to nut being so charged up watching Tim being fucked at both ends. When he did, he wiped his slick cock on Tim's cock and balls and let an Irish construction worker take Tim's ass. The Irishmen wasn't in a hurry. He shoved his cock in, took out a cigarette and lit it.

"Good day ta ya laddie. Mind if I take a piss in this hot hole of yours?"

Tim of course couldn't say anything, but Sarge told him to go right ahead, it needed a good cleaning out anyway.

The drill instructor pulled his dick out and scooted up so that both his tree trunk legs were now on each side of Tim's face.

"Get your tongue working in my ass sailor. You hear me? I want to fell that tongue of yours working in my ass crack sailor."

Tim's neck careened up. His tongue drove into the crack of the drill instructor.

Sarge picked up a match on the table and struck it. He then re-lit his chewed on cigar and flicked the used match on the floor. After a few puffs on the cigar, Sarge reached behind him and grabbed Tim by his blond curly hair and yanked the sailor's face into his butt crack.

"Get in there sailor and lick that sweaty fucking crack of mine. Did you hear me boy. Get your tongue to work!"

Tim's eyes bulged out as he tried to get more of his tongue between the two melons of Sarge's butt. The sailor's nose was buried in the hot moist crack and Sarge's ass hairs were tickling the end of Tim's sniffer.

The sailor tasted all of the salty rank sweat the drill sergeant had in his crack. His tongue went up and down the crack and deep inside, grazing Sarge's butt-hole. It was like nectar to a hummingbird and Tim's tongue slurped it and brought it back to his mouth before reaching out and slurping more of the hot stinking sweat of Sarge's moist crack. Tim's tongue cleaned all the ass hairs on its travel from one end of the butt crack to the other. It dove down deep when he neared the butt-hole and wiped it cleaned of sweat and butt juice.

The Irishman pounded Tim's ass. He drove deep into the sailor's butt and caused Tim's head to jerk as he ate Sarge's butthole.

Sarge backed away from Tim's tongue and shoved his cock back in the sailor's mouth. He held it there and allowed the Irishman to hammer Tim's ass as he pumped the sailor's mouth with his cock.

"Ah it feels better than Father O'Malley's mouth on my dick." The Irishman proclaimed.

Sarge yelled at the Irishman, "I would think it would. That's Navy ass you're fucking there Patty. You can't find a better fuck than that."

"Never a truer word was spoken," the Irishman said before he slammed the ass one last time and shot his load deep in the sailor's gut.

Once Tim's hole was vacated, Sarge pulled out of his mouth and moved the men aside to plug the sailor's ass again. Piss and cum dripped out of the hairless hole of the sailor. The tight rosebud burped and spewed butt juice onto the floor.

"Jesus, sailor, I think they filled your guts up with spooge and piss. Bull?"

"Yeah Sarge."

"Throw me that butt-plug on the counter will ya."

"Sure Sarge."

Bull tossed the plug by using the jock strap to swing it in the air. Sarge caught it and shoved it in the sailor's hole to plug it. Then he reached over and pulled on the sailor's pant legs and brought them down to the floor. Sarge grabbed Tim's arm and helped him to sit up. Once the sailor was sitting, Sarge took the jock and placed it over Tim's face so that his mouth and nose was buried in the pouch. "Ya better get in the head sailor before you pull that plug out. When you're ready for duty, report back to me."

"Aye aye Sir," Tim said through the meshed jock and shuffled to the men's room with his pants around his ankles and the jock on his face.

Sarge walked back to the bar and poured another drink for him and the sailor. He watched the men in the bar, some went back to playing cards, others talked among themselves and laid side bets. A couple more construction men walked in and ordered drinks from Bull.

Sarge pulled out a wad of money and turned to Madame Woo.

"You got a nice room for us," He asked.

Madame Woo looked briefly at the marine's bankroll before she sucked on her cigarette holder and blew a smoke ring.

"I have number eight all ready for you Sarge. Your favorite, isn't that right?"

"Thanks Woo. Here's a couple bills to cover it."

Sarge peeled off some bills from the wad of money and handed it to Woo, who quickly took the cash and secreted it away in her silk dress.

Tim came out of the head and shuffled over to where Sarge stood by the bar. The men in the bar looked at the sailor with his pants around his ankles and a black butt-plug stuck in his ass. The bar crowd grabbed at their crotches and winked as he shuffled by.

"You all cleaned out and ready for another round sailor?"

Tim smiled and pushed a lock of blond hair from his eyes. "I'm ready Sarge!"

"Good sailor. You're clean as a whistle?"

"Sir. Yes Sir. Reporting for duty sir."

"Good sailor. Bend over."

Tim turned around and bent over. He could feel Sarge grab the butt-plug and yank it out. By now he was use to feeling large objects shoved in and out of his ass and hardly flinched when the plug was removed.

Sarge slammed the plug back on the bar top and took the jock off of Tim's face. He placed it back on the plug and poured the whiskey he had for Tim on the jock.

"Better get to suckin' that jock sailor, if you want your whiskey."

Tim happily went to town on the soaked jockstrap, sucking out as much whiskey as he could. His ass was bent over and Sarge saw the opportunity to slam his barracuda back in.

"Feels like that baby-maker of mine is back home. Don't it Sailor Boy."

"Feels good to me Sarge. You gonna fuck me some more?"

"Whadda think I'm doin' now sailor?"

"Ya fucking me good Sarge."

"That's right sailor. You were made to be fuck weren't ya."

"Sir. Yes sir, Sarge."

Sarge got real close to Tim with his cock all the way in the sailor's ass. He reached around the sailor and began to play with the nubs of his nipples as the sailor sucked on the jock pouch, getting all the whiskey he could from it.

Sarge put his mouth right next to the sailor's ear and whispered, "Yeah sailor, you like that big fucking dick of mine in you. Don't ya. You like it when I play with your nubs, huh. I know you do sailor, I can feel that hot ass of yours grinding back for all the cock it can get."

Tim stopped sucking for a moment and said, "I want you to fuck me all the time Sarge. I love having that cock of yours in me. I love just holding it and giving it kisses. I love your cock Sarge. I need it all the time."

"I know you do sailor, and I'm gonna give you all the dick you ever wanted. You'd like that sailor? Like to have my cock in you all the time?"

"Yeah Sarge. Give me all the dick you can. I love it Sarge."

"I thought you would say that sailor. You fuckin' little slut. Are you a slut sailor? Want me to whore you out to the troops? Wanna suck cock? Take dick up your ass for me Sailor Boy?"

"Yeah, Sarge. Give me dick Sarge. Give me all the cock I can have."

"You're a greedy fuckin' pig, aren't you Sailor Boy. A greedy fucking dick pig."

"Yes sir, Sarge. I'm your cock pig sir."

"You bet you are sailor. I own that ass and mouth of yours. Don't I sailor? Don't I?"

"Yes sir. Sergeant Sir. You own my sailor ass and mouth, sir."

"You bet I do sailor. You bet your sweet fuckin' ass I own you. Now get your mouth back on that butt-plug and suck that fuckin' jock pouch bitch."

"Sir. Yes sir."

Tim went back to sucking on the jock pouch and Sarge went back to dick slamming the sailor.

CHAPTER FOUR

"Bull!" yelled one of the marines playing poker. Get Suit out here, will ya?"

"Sure." Bull turned around and kicked a kneeling man in the balls that was dressed in a suit and tie crouched under the bar's top. "Get the fuck out there and make yourself useful, ass-wipe."

The prissy office worker looked up at Bull with big blue eyes. A lock of light brown hair fell on his forehead, from an otherwise perfect hair-cut. Suit wore a smart tie to compliment the dark, blue-gray jacket and pants. The cuff of his sleeve showed a bit, and he wore expensive dress shoes. Clean-shaven, he looked like he just got up from a board meeting rather than at the feet of Bull.

Suit hurried to the marine, knelt next to him and opened his mouth as wide as he could. The marine hocked a loogie into Suit's waiting mouth. Suit's eyes looked around to see if anyone else needed a spittoon and saw another marine on the other side of the table with a cigar that had some ash about to fall. He hurried to other side, the marine tapped the cigar on Suit's opened mouth, and the ash fell in.

Suit then put his hand up with his fingers in the form of a V. The marine snug his cigar in the offered holder and Suit held it over his opened mouth as his big blue eyes looked around the room in case anyone needed a spittoon or an ashtray.

When the marine picked up his cigar again, another marine grabbed Suit by his hair and dragged him over to the table where Tim was being fucked at both ends.

"Clean this shit up, ass-wipe," he said.

Suit obediently licked the floor of all the cum, piss and cock juice that he could find, and then begged the marine if he could clean his cock as well.

"Fuck you dirt-bag. You just wanna suck my dick don't ya?"

"Sir, please sir."

"I wouldn't let a scumbag like you near my dick." The marine kicked Suit in the balls and sent him flying. He lay in a ball and groaned holding his nuts.

The soldier with the cigar that Suit was holding before he was forced to clean the floor with his tongue, called him.

"Get your fucking worthless ass back here."

Suit crawled back to the marine. "Sir. Yes sir."

"Did I tell you to leave?"

"Sir. No sir."

"Stop playing with yourself you dumb shit."

"Sir. Yes sir,"

Suit removed his hands from his balls and as soon as he did, the marine gave him a harder kick to the nuts. Suit rolled over groaning and holding on his crotch.

"Stop playing with yourself you fuckin' pervert and make yourself useful."

Breathless, Suit managed to say, "Sir. Yes sir and crawled over to the marine. The big marine sucked on the end of the cigar and then blew the smoke right in Suits face.

"Open your fuckin' toilet mouth ass-hole."

Suit opened his mouth wide and the marine took the cigar and knocked the ash in Suit's mouth. Then he hocked a loogie on top of the ash. Another wad of spit hit him between the eyes. Suit raised his hand up to hold the marine's cigar and kept the ash and spit in his mouth with it still open.

"What a good for nothing piece of shit you are." The marine said before he went back to play cards.

Sarge was getting ready to nut. He slammed the sailor's ass and ground his big ole fucker deep in the boy's plump little butt. When Sarge came, it seeped out around Tim's ass lips and dripped on the floor into a puddle of jizz.

Sarge yelled once he calmed down after the last squirt deep in the sailor's guts. "Suit!" he yelled out.

The marine playing poker picked up his cigar and Suit ran next to Sarge, knelling. Sarge took the chewed cigar butt in his clenched teeth; the end mashed and wet with spit from Sarge and dropped it in Suit's mouth.

The kneeling man chewed it and swallowed.

Sarge grabbed the sailor and hugged him close to his body. His meaty cock still lodged deep in the sailor's butt. Taking the sloppy, piss stained jock off the butt-plug; he draped it over Suit's head. The pouch covered his mouth, nose, and eyes. Sarge then picked up the butt-plug and worked it into the sailor's mouth, which took some effort.

Tim's mouth could hardly stretch open for the width of the butt-plug, and when he finally did, he sucked it in with the end obscenely stuck out of his mouth, the flange of the butt-plug covering his lips.

"That will get that mouth of yours stretched out like your ass-pussy sailor. You'll be sucking Sarge's cock for a while."

He held the sailor up with his dick stuffed in the boy's butt while Tim's feet dangled off the floor.

Looking down at Suit, Sarge spit on the jock pouch that covered Suit's face and said, "Clean up this shit, ya stupid fuck," and then kicked Suit in the nuts.

Suit groaned and put his face to the floor slurping up the butt juice and jizz that had dripped from Sarge's ass fucking.

Sarge left Suit to his cleaning, and cocked-walked the sailor to the stairs and up to the room Madame Woo had waiting for him. Tim's legs dangled with Sarge's cock embedded deep in his ass with the sailor's pants bunched around his ankles. Sarge held on to the sailor's nipples and Tim sucked on the butt-plug like a baby on a pacifier as he was cocked-walked.

The marines went back to their game and the longshoremen ordered more beer, pulling on their dicks that had hardened in their pants.

Sarge cocked-walked Tim down the narrow dark hallway and then stopped at a door labeled with the number eight.

"Open the door Sailor Boy," Sarge whispered in Tim's ear.

The sailor reached out with a hand, his butt stuffed with marine cock, and opened the door. Sarge walked him in and with a back kick, shut the door.

The marine started to bounce the sailor on his cock while still holding on to his nipples and talked in his ear as the sailor sucked the butt plug.

"I got another present for you sweet stuff. You gonna love it but ya gotta be a real fuckin' slut to get it. You a slut, Sailor Boy? You wanna ride my fuck-stick and whore for me?"

Tim tried to talk around the butt-plug in his mouth; he leaned his head back on Sarge's shoulder and nodded, his eyes looking imploringly at Sarge.

"That's a good boy."

Sarge lifted the sailor off his cock and threw him on the bed. He walked over to a dressing table where a bottle of whiskey and two glasses were on top and said to Tim, as he poured the booze. "Get your clothes off sailor."

Tim began to strip and throw his uniform on the floor. The brass bed bounced with his maneuvering as his clothes fell to the oriental carpet underneath. All the while, Tim sucked the butt-plug while watching Sarge take the two glasses with the bottle of whiskey and walk to an overstuffed, threadbare chair. Sarge put the shot glasses with the bottle on a small wood table next to the chair and watched as Tim pulled off the last of his clothes.

"Shove that plug up your ass," Sarge barked.

Tim pulled the plug out of his mouth, placed it on his butt-hole, and shoved it in. The sailor's mouth looked bigger around than it did before. His lips were puffy and stretched.

"Come over here," Sarge commanded.

Tim got off the bed and walked toward Sarge. The only light in the room came from a dim bulb inside a silk, red lantern that hung over Sarge.

When the sailor stood in front of Sarge he said to the sailor, "Spread your legs."

The sailor spread his legs, his stiff cock sticking straight out, his balls hung low in their sack. Sarge took a fresh cigar from his shirt pocket. After lighting it, he blew the smoke in the sailor's face, reached out, and grabbed the hanging nut-sack.

Sarge tugged on them, twisted them, and slapped the sailor's cock, making it goo from its dick-slit.

"Nice fuckin' balls. Not a feather on them."

"Thanks Sarge. Fuck Sarge, I'm gonna cum if you keep playing with my nuts like that."

"Wouldn't that be a shame," Sarge said with a grin.

Sarge pulled the balls down and with his other hand, slapped the distended nuts. He looked at where he slapped the balls and then slapped them some more, one side and then the other.

The sailor's cock spurted goo, crystal clear and slimy. "Fuck. Shit motherfucking, Sarge you gonna make me cum. Shit. Jesus-Fucking-Christ!"

Tim watched Sarge suck on his cigar. The tip glowed red for a moment before a cloud of smoke blew on his face. The sailor looked down at his cock jumping around, spitting cock snot at the end that covered his legs and stomach. It also covered Sarge's steel-hard arm and the fingers that tightly squeezed around his sack, forcing his nuts down tight. Each smack from Sarge's hand caused his cock to fling out more cock-snot.

Sarge stopped slapping Tim's nuts, took the cigar from his mouth and placed it on the metal ashtray on the table.

The marine used one hand to hold Tim's nuts out and with other grabbed the head of Tim's cock and milked it for its slime. With his hand slicked up, he massaged the goop on Tim's nuts while pulling on them.

"You like that sailor? You like that mother-fucker?"

Tim's hands played with his nipples, making the nibs hard and sticking an inch out. His head lobbed around and his legs began to shake. "Shit, fucking shit. I'm fucking goin' to cum. Fucking, shit mother-fucker!"

"Come you fucker, Come on. Blow that fucker. Come on." Sarge sped up rubbing Tim's nuts with one hand as he pulled the sack down with the other.

Tim groaned, he whimpered. His asshole sucked on the butt-plug, the flange of the plug fought against Tim's ass trying to engulf it. His muscled abs popped out like a washboard and when his eyelashes began to flutter, he shot a load of spunk, and moaned long and deep.

Sarge kept pulling on the nut-sack. He told Tim to blow his fucking wad while the sailor spunked and shot out volleys of jizz.

Tim's cock shot repeatedly as it swung above Sarge's hands that pulled on the nut-sack. It shot all over Tim, the floor, and Sarge before the cock went semi-soft and dripped semen like a spider's web, to the floor.

"Yeah, mother-fucker. Got you off good didn't I?"

The sailor groaned and opened his eyes, "You sure did Sarge. I haven't come since the last we got together."

"I can see, and I'm gonna give you something for being such a good boy."

The sergeant picked up his cigar and gave it a few puffs, expelling the smoke in the sailor's face before sitting it back down in the ashtray. Reaching into his pant pocket, he took out a stainless steel cylinder about five inches long.

"We're gonna add a little weight to them balls of yours. Make'm hang real good."

Sarge told Tim to get one of the shoelaces from his shoes. When the sailor came back and handed the shoelace to Sarge, the sergeant grabbed one of Tim's nuts and tied one end of the shoelace to it. He then put the loose end in the cylinder until it dangled out the other side where he grabbed it and pulled.

Tim's face contorted but he held firm. Sarge then took the shoelace off and did the same thing with the other nut. This time the sailor almost doubled over when the nut was yanked through the steel cylinder.

Sarge held the nuts in his hand and looked at his handiwork.

"Later on I might get you a bigger one, say ten pounds of steel. This here bad-boy is only five, but it's gonna keep your nuts nice and loose. I'll show ya how to shove-em up your ass later on."

He let go of the balls, the weight dropped pulling Tim's nuts down, and then Sarge slapped them to make them swing.

"What do you think sailor? Like your present?"

Tim looked down between his spread legs at his nuts and its steel ball weight, and watched them swing. His dick started to get hard again.

"Man Sarge, that feels fuckin' great. At first I wasn't so sure, but shit it's turning me on again."

The sailor tweaked one of his nipples and with the other hand, played with the butt-plug in his ass while he watched his balls swing back and forth with Sarge's hand smacking them.

The sailor looked at Sarge and pleaded, "Fuck Sarge, let me suck your cock. Please?"

Sarge slapped the steel ball weight again and watched them swing back hitting the sailors butt-plug stuck in his ass and then swing forward.

"Well maybe I will, while I smoke my cigar."

Sarge spread his legs as he sat back in the chair. The sailor got on his knees with his legs spread, the butt-plug deep in his gut.

The marine's cock hung between his spread thighs, over his ball-sack pooled in the chair, the head of the cock dangled over the side of the cushion Sarge sat in. The cock's piss slit stared at Tim like a one-eyed monster waiting for the salvia dripping mouth of the sailor. The sergeant stared down at the sailor kneeling at his feet.

Tim's legs were spread so Sarge could kick the ball weight and hear it smack the rubber plug buried in the sailor's butt, and the sailor's dick slapped against the top of Sarge's boot when he did.

Sarge picked up the cigar and put it back in his mouth. He watched as the sailor engulfed the head of his dick. Tim's eyes focused on Sarge's face, his lips stretched obscenely around the sergeant's big fat dick. The sergeant reached over and poured himself another shot of whiskey, looked down again before taking a sip and smacked the sailor's weighted nuts. He listened to them hit the plug and felt sailor's dick slap the top of his boot. It made Tim suck deeper on the dong lodged in his mouth. Tim swallowed Sarge's python down his throat, swelling out his neck with the girth of the marine's dick. Sarge's cock began to harden as he thought about enjoying this for a while. And as the sailor sucked, the marine sipped his whiskey, smoked his cigar, and smacked Tim's balls with his boot.

CHAPTER FIVE

Madame Woo looked around. The boys were getting along fine. Playing cards, talking, groping each other and Suit was busy filling orders of whiskey and beer when he wasn't being used for an ashtray or spittoon. She sipped her Mai Tai and thought of going to her room for a bit of opium before Sarge came back with Sailor Boy. She knew that at some point, Sarge would be down and the house would be full of activity she didn't want to miss. She just put out her cigarette when the beaded curtain on the front door moved and a cop peered in.

"Evening Madame Woo," the officer said and tipped his hat.

"Sergeant O'Reilly, you looking for bad guys?" she chortled.

The sergeant stepped in, and with him came three other squared-jawed officers. All of them well built and dressed in tight uniforms that bulged at the right places. Madame Woo noticed that their pants sported boners. She could see the outline of their cocks through the uniforms. Madame Woo thought it looked as if they had been working out, their chests and arms ripped at the fabric.

"Well ma'am. If we were, you wouldn't be hiding any criminals here, now would you?"

"Oh, no sergeant. I run clean joint. You know that." She giggled and reached out with one of her long fingernails and tickled the sergeant's crotch.

The officer blushed and grabbed his dick, giving it a pull.

"Well, I'm not sure. We might have to look around. Just to make sure everything is in order."

"Okay sergeant. Maybe you and your men might like a drink, to keep out the cold. On the house of course."

"Well, that be nice of you Madame Woo but we're on duty and it wouldn't be right."

"I won't tell anyone sergeant. You know me. I half blind from old age."

"Oh, I think you've seen plenty Madame Woo. Plenty."

"Well, maybe so. But my memory gets cloudy with the smoke of so many years. Let me have Suit wait on you, while you and your men relax before going."

"Well, maybe for just a short while. A wee scotch for the fog that's rolling in."

"Very good sergeant. Bull?"

"Yes, ma'am"

"Have Suit assist officers."

"Sure will Madame Woo."

Madame Woo reached her hand out to the officer and took him by the arm.

"I'm going to retire. It will be a long night and I don't want to miss it. Sarge and Sailor Boy are upstairs."

The sergeant helped her down from the stool and escorted her to the stairs. She looked up with glee at his face to see the response her news brought.

Sergeant O'Reilly beamed. His rosy cheeks seemed rosier and the dimple in his chin almost had a grin to match his smile.

As Madame Woo ascended the stairs, the police officer tipped his hat. "Have a nice lie down and I'll tell the boys the good news."

Madame Woo thought she might have a pipe of opium now that the cops were here, she knew the men would be less likely to get in a knife fight and break up the furniture. The furniture worried her the most.

O'Reilly walked backed to the bar where his men were talking with Bull. One of the officers had the heel of his boot planted on Suit's face. The groveling man's tongue lapped as best it could at the leather heel.

"Sarge is here with Sailor Boy," The sergeant said when he got to the bar.

"That right Bull?" Asked one of the cops.

"They're upstairs. I imagine Sarge is teaching Sailor Boy some new tricks."

"That a fact," said the cop whose foot rested on Suit's face and then moved his boot back and forth on the lapping tongue.

"How about a wee bit of scotch, Bull?"

"Sure thing O'Reilly."

Bull reached for one of the bottles on the back wall of the bar and poured the officer a full glass.

"Well I suppose we'll have to entertain ourselves here for bit. Won't we boys?"

"It looks that way," said the youngest looking cop who was rubbing his crotch and looking around the bar.

Two men were in a corner talking softly. One of them had his hand inside the shirt of the other, playing with the ring in his nipple. A construction worker was on his knees giving a blow-job to a dockworker and the marines, playing cards, had parts of their uniforms off, apparently from a game of strip poker.

The cop who had Suit cleaning his boots now had him working the sides and top of his boots with his tongue. He took his baton and tapped on Suit's head.

"Shit-head."

"Sir?"

"Open yer fuckin' mouth."

Suit immediately opened his mouth and the officer spat. It hit Suit's nose and cheek and Suit's tongue came out and licked the spit on his face before he went back to lapping at the boots. Another officer picked up his drink and in one swallow, downed the whole glass of whiskey. "Maybe I better check out the head. Might be some illegal activity going on in there," he said as he pulled on the bulge in his crotch.

"Let us know if you need help," another officer said with a laugh as the cop walked toward the bathroom. When he entered, a construction worker and a dock man followed him.

The younger looking cop walked over to the two men in the corner and O'Reilly turned to talk with the officer whose boots were being cleaned by Suit's tongue.

"So, Wolfe, I heard you beat that complaint about messing up that burglar you caught last month."

Wolfe ran a finger over a scar on his cheek. "After I had a talk with that little ass-hole, he told the captain he fell down the stairs and was just trying to make trouble for me. He recanted the whole story he made up."

"I remember he didn't sit very much after that."

"I think it was the whip I used in our little talk that made him, let's say, uneasy in an easy chair."

"The boys in the jail house said he's their best prisoner. Never says a damn thing except, yes sir and no sir."

"Yeah, after they have a talk with me, they seem to settle down real fast."

Wolfe grabbed his crotch and squeezed. "I remember in our conversation that he said he wasn't any one's cocksucker and he wasn't about to be one to a god-damn cop either. Hah! That fucker was sucking like a damn vacuum cleaner in ten fuckin' minutes after he said that. I had him eat the words too, once he spelled them right after cleaning my asshole."

Wolfe looked down at Suit at work and said, "You better get to work on O'Reilly's boots boy, if you don't want to feel my baton. You hear me boy? Are you listening to me you stupid fuck?"

"Sir. Yes sir. Right away sir."

Suit jumped to O'Reilly's boots and his tongue slathered at the leather wherever he thought there might be any dirt.

Wolfe picked up his foot and slammed it down on the back of Suit's head, smashing his face into O'Reilly's leathered boot.

"Clean it mother-fucker. Get some spit going and clean his god-damn fuckin' boots, ass-wipe."

Suit responded by doubling his effort, his tongue darted all over the officers boots, lapped at the edges of the soles where they met the floor. He took long tongue strokes across the grain and up the sides of the leather as sweat poured from his forehead and puddle around the boots.

Wolfe turned to O'Reilly once he saw Suit comply. "These fuckin' dirt-bags. If you don't keep on them, they just get lazier by the minute."

O'Reilly looked down at Suit's administrations, "Well he sure is busy now, look at the tongue work. We could set up a shoe shine spot for him at the police station. Wouldn't need to buff them after patrol, with a tongue like that at work on them."

"I like them naked myself. This bastard is too well dressed. Give them old worn out jocks that's too damn raunchy to wear anymore and that's all scum like him needs to wear."

"Ya wouldn't be able to call him Suit if ya did," said O'Reilly.

"Why call him anything but scumbag. That's good enough for the likes of this ass-hole."

O'Reilly looked down at Suit. "Hey ass-hole."

Suit looked up but still kept his tongue busy.

"Dip-shit. Fucker. Dick-breath."

Suit kept his eyes on the officer and his tongue on the boots.

"Ya see there," O'Reilly said turning back to Wolfe, "This ass-sucker doesn't care what you call him. Ain't that right piss-breath."

Suit stared back at O'Reilly and nodded his head in agreement but kept his tongue on the boot.

"Ya know O'Reilly, if I had some rope I could try out some new knots on this ass-hole."

"Laddie, that's a fine an idea as I heard all day." O'Reilly looked at Bull and asked, "Do you have any rope by chance, Bull?"

Bull smiled and said, "Matter of fact, I do."

The beefy bartender went to the back of the bar. Hanging from a hook was roped coiled up on a nail. He took it down and walked back to the two officers and gave the rope to Wolfe.

The officer grabbed the rope, took one end and pulled hard with both hands. The rope snapped.

"Good rope you got there Bull. I bet this hemp could hang a man by the balls. What do you think O'Reilly?"

The officer took the rope and felt the weight. "Shit you could string two men up with this rope and use them to swing on."

Bull looked at the two cops and said, "Well there's only one way to find out. Isn't there? You can use that timber there in front of the bar." Bull said as he pointed up to the cross beams that ran the length of the room.

Wolfe smiled for the first time. He walked over to the beam and tossed the end of the rope over, like a master rope-man, it came down on the other side of the beam. He pulled on the end until the length was even on both sides.

"Now let's see. Who could we use, O'Reilly. Know any ass-hole dumb enough to let us tie him?"

"Shit Wolfe. That would have to be a pretty dumb mother-fucker. Hey, dick-breath?"

Suit looked up at O'Reilly as he licked the top of the boot.

"Are you as dumb as shit?"

Suit nodded.

"You are? Jesus, I never thought anybody could be that fuckin' stupid. Wolfe! Ass-hole here said he loved to be hog-tied."

"No kidding. Dip-shit, get off the fuckin' floor, get those filthy fucking clothes off and come here."

Suit jumped up. He immediately began undressing.

Bull screamed at Suit, "Jesus fucking Christ. Don't take your fucking rags off here ass-hole. Go behind the bar where you keep your fucking jock collection and change."

Bull turned to O'Reilly as Suit ran behind the bar. "That fuckin' fag has the filthiest fucking jock straps you've ever seen. Treats them like treasure. How fucked up can you be?"

"Fuckin' degenerate. You know we better teach him a lesson. Fag shit like that. Where the hell does he get them?"

"In the can. He's always sneakin off to clean the urinal trough. Fucker bathes in it. I can hear him beg from here for a guy's jock. Always asking to sniff it, and chew it up a bit and get all the crust and shit off it. Fuck, some of those construction guys got the nastiest fucking jocks. Guess they never heard you don't need to wear them until they fall off. Put a fresh one on the first of the month like everyone else."

O'Reilly leaned over the bar and saw Suit stack his clothes on top a pile of yellowed, sweat, piss and cum encrusted jock straps. "Jesus," he said with a look of disgust.

"Suit pays them twenty bucks a jock. Good thing he has a day job at some law firm up town."

Suit came running from behind the bar bare-ass naked and stood in front of Wolfe.

"Hey Wolfe! Can you work some of his jock straps in? I'd hate to think of him missing his toys," Bull yelled.

"Look fuck-up. Why the fuck didn't you bring some of your god-damn fucking jocks out here? Son-of-a-bitch. Get your fucking ass moving, and you better bring the filthiest fucking jocks I ever saw, or I'll fuckin' kick your ass to Jesus."

Suit turned whiter than he already was and ran back to the bar, jumped to the ground, and rummaged through a pile of jocks.

"What the fuck is taking you so long, maggot?"

Suit scurried from behind the bar and ran with his hands full of jocks to face Wolfe.

"Jesus fucking Christ. You fucking pervert. Those are the nastiest fuckin' things I've ever seen. Christ."

The smell from the jocks permeated the room. Bull lit one of the incense sticks Madame Woo kept on hand and stuck it in the iron caldron.

"Start shoving them in your mouth fuck-head."

Suit took a jock and shoved it in his mouth. As soon as he had most of it in, he took another one and shoved it in his mouth. He kept on mouthing the jocks and picking another one to force in.

Wolfe stared at him, un-amused.

Suit kept trying to stuff more jocks in. He looked pleadingly at Wolfe but saw no reaction.

As he forced another jock, the straps still sticking out of his mouth, Wolfe put his gloves on and grabbed the rest of the jocks from Suit's hand. "You fucking stupid shit," he said and jammed the whole handful in Suit's mouth. He was gagging on them. His cheeks bulged out tight, his lips unable to meet because his mouth was stretched as wide as the skin would allow.

"You fuckin sissy. When I tell you to eat the fuckin' jocks. You fucking eat them. Not like some goddamn girl at a fuckin' tea party."

O'Reilly turned to Bull, "That fucker is asking for it. Dumb as a fuckin' post."

Suit's prick was rock hard and hairless. He was required by Bull to shave every hair off except for his head, in case it was needed to pull on. Suit's body was muscled but thin from all the shit detail he had to perform at the bar. His blue eyes were always darting here and there, to see if he was needed in any way and his dick was always hard no matter how much punishment he took.

"Chew the jocks ass-hole. I want them softened up. Shit I never seen such piss and cum encrusted jocks in all my life!" exclaimed Wolfe.

Suit did his best at mashing the jocks stuffed in his mouth. All he could do was to mash down and the phlegm he gagged up helped to lubricate the crusty jocks. The odor of an overflowing urinal permeated his nostrils and reacted as amyl to his brain.

"Stop chewing like it was cud, ya fucking shit-for-brains. Open your fucking mouth."

As best as Suit tried to open his mouth further, it could not, and Wolfe reached between Suit's teeth with his leather gloved hand and pulled two out. It helped Suit some to chew.

"Stop fucking off, ass-wipe and put one jock on and the other on your head."

Suit quickly stepped into the jock and pulled it up. He then took the other jock and pulled it over his head with the pouch over his eyes, mouth and nose.

"Now chew a hole in the pouch for my fucking dick."

Suit grabbed at the pouch with his lips and pulled some of the jock-pouch in his mouth. He could barely reach it with his front teeth.

Wolfe got real close to Suit and looked down at him. "Well?"

Suit chewed as fast as a squirrel. Nibbling like a rat on the mesh cloth.

"Jesus fucking Christ. Ass-hole, how long is it going to take?"

Suit began to sweat, he started to swallow one of the jocks lodged deep in back of his mouth and felt the straps slide down his throat. It gave him a little more room, with a yank, the half rotted pouch tore.

Wolfe looked at the hole. "Good enough, I don't have all fuckin' night for you to chew a decent fucking hole in a jock. Why I thought such a dumb mother-fucker as you could do anything that simple just shows how grateful you should be that I don't beat the living shit out of you."

Suit did his best to answer, but it sounded like a grunt through all the jocks still in his mouth.

"Fucking pig." Wolfe turned to Bull and O'Reilly with his back to Suit.

"I just told him I was going to beat him for not doing things right and he fucking grunts at me."

"Fucking cock-sucker," said O'Reilly. "Are you going to let him get away with that shit?"

Wolfe turned back to Suit and backhanded him. The blow sent Suit to the floor and Suit crawled to Wolfe's boots put his head to the floor and raised his ass. The yellow piss stained straps of the jock outlined the two creamy ass cheeks. His tight little pucker now opened like a rosebud.

Wolfe walked behind him and spat at the pucker. Than he turned and sat on the haunches of Suit's ass-end. Using Suit as a stool he slapped the upturned ass. First one gloved hand and the then the other. Suit's butt was a glowing red before Wolfe stopped and when he did, he took four fingers and shoved them in Suit's ass. Wolfe reamed him good, finger fucking Suit's butt until the black leather of his gloves glistened.

Once Wolfe was done abusing Suit's ass, he stood and told Suit to hand him one end of the rope. Wolfe grabbed the rope and proceeded to tie up Suits cock and balls with the jock still on. When he was finished, Suit's genitals stuck up in a tight ball confined in the mesh of the jock. Coils of rope around the base of the cock and balls pushed them out further as the mesh held them confined.

Wolfe roped each ankle before going back to Suit's stuffed jock pouch. He pulled the rope tight so that the pouch, full of cock and balls, pulled down between Suit's legs. Wolfe then took the rope and hoisted Suit's legs in the air. Now his head and shoulders were on the ground and his legs and ass were in the air. The pouch of the jock stuck out like a balloon between Suit's legs. Wolfe walked to Suit putting his feet on each side of Suit's head. He reached for the other end of the rope and pulled enough out to work with.

"Cough up one of them jocks ass-hole and hand it to me."

Suit complied and pulled a jock from his mouth handing it to Wolfe who strung one end of the rope through one leg strap and the other end of rope through the other leg strap.

"Another."

Suit handed him another jock from his mouth and Wolfe did the same thing until there were five or six jocks strung between the two rope ends.

When Wolfe was done he had tied each of Suit's arms to the ends of the rope and hoisted the ropes over the beam. Suit was tied in a hammock of jocks, his legs spread and up at one end, his head hung back the other with his arms pulled up and his cock and balls encased in a jock pouch and tied up with his feet. Like a self made harness of rope and jocks. Suit now looked at the room upside down with his head falling back, perfect to shove a cock deep in his throat. His ass was open and the pouch of tied up genitals were ready to pull and skewer a dick deep in his ass.

Suit was now tied up and trussed with his head hanging back and a stinking jockstrap over his mouth. Wolfe walked over to where Suit had his mouth open and took out his dick. It was huge, mean looking. The veins wound around his cock and pulsed with blood, filling up the engorged cock. He lit a cigarette and threw the match into the hole in the jock covered mouth. Then he took his cock and held it so that the head hung down just inches from the hole in the jock and began to piss. Smoke came out of the mouth from the match being drowned. Piss flowed and bubbled up while Suit desperately tried to swallow. Wolfe smoked his cigarette and peed. Once he was through pissing, he dropped the cigarette in the mouth hole and Suit swallowed the last of the piss with the butt of the cigarette, like a toilet being flushed.

Wolfe walked back to the ass end, grabbed the rope attached to Suit's balls and pulled. Suit's ass embedded itself on Wolfe's cock. A groan came out of the mouth hole and Wolfe started to swing the trussed up balls back and forth, screwing the ass deeper and harder on his dick.

The slave began to moan until Wolfe backhanded the tied up balls with a hard slap. That got a yelp out of Suit.

"O'Reilly!"

"Yeah Wolfe?"

"Stick something in that asshole's mouth will ya."

"Be glad too."

The Irish cop walked over to the head of Suit. He pulled out his big fat un-cut cock and began to dick slap the jock covered face before he slammed it into the hole of the pouch shoving until the zipper of his fly ground against the mesh of the jock.

The meaty dick swelled out Suit's throat. His eyes watered while they stared up at the uniformed ass above him. The slave had a worried look, as if he wondered how long the officer would have his throat stuffed with hot cop dick.

Wolfe plummet the stretched out balls. The cop smacked Suit's nuts with his hand on one side and then the other until they swelled. Every time he slapped them, Suit's asshole would pucker from the stab of pain in his nuts and Wolfe loved the feel of the tight butt-hole when it would spasm on his dick.

When Suit's nuts stopped responding to the slaps, Wolfe reached out and squeezed them in his hand until he felt the sphincter grip his dick again. Every time the butt-hole relaxed, Wolfe squeezed harder until Suit's guts began to tighten and he retched on the dick shoved down this throat.

"Damn if that don't feel good." O'Reilly said.

"What feels good?" asked Wolfe as he fucked the ass and squeezed the nut sack.

"Whatever you're doing to him, this hot gush comes up from his gut and covers my dick in his throat."

"What a fuckin cock-sucker. He must have a pussy for a mouth," said Wolfe.

"It's a sight better than my wife's. He smells like a urinal, the old lady stinks like three old day fish."

Wolfe squeezed the balls with a twist. "Maybe I should hang him by the nuts. Forget the rope. Bet that pucker of his would stay good and tight then."

"I'll tell ya, he's loosey-goosey now. Jaw is slacked. Maybe I'll pull it out some and give him a breather."

O'Reilly started to withdraw his dick from the hole in the pouch. Inch by inch of cock meat snaked from the gapping mouth before there was a rush of air, as Suit's lungs filled with breath.

It wasn't for long however. O'Reilly began to piss once his dick's head was at Suit's lips. It foamed over, soaking the pouch and dripped on the floor.

Suit gurgled and coughed like a drowning man. The stream went on as Wolfe shoved his cock in and out of the ass and now, used his fist on the tortured nuts.

Suit's eyes were wild. He could only see things up-side down and for the most part, the crotch of O'Reilly's pants. And that's where his eyes focused. Where the crack of the cop's ass was outlined by the tight cloth stretched over it. The fabric formed over the two melons of ass and up the crack as if almost painted on. He could almost make out where the hole would be and how his tongue would fit nicely in the crack.

Whack!

Suit's body convulsed, Wolfe had his baton out and was ready to strike another blow to the beaten balls in his fist.

Whack!

A deep low groan came from around the dick in Suit's mouth.

"Fuck yeah, I'm shootin' now," bellowed Wolfe just before he struck the balls a third time with his baton.

"Fuck. That's good. Yeah, you fuckin' piece of shit take it!"

Wolfe planted his cock deep in the bowels of Suit and held on as his prick shot load after load of cum deep in his guts.

O'Reilly shoved his meat back in and slapped Suit's pissed on face. He grabbed the cocksucker's throat and felt his dick plunging pass the Adam apple.

"You fuckin' dick wad. Eat my fuck stick cocksucker. Eat my fuckin' dick." O'Reilly said as he brought the tempo up of his dick fucking the hot throat.

Suit struggled to breath. His hands grasped at the air, his lungs grabbed any breath they could find between the thrusts made down his cock-sucking throat.

O'Reilly held still, his hands tightened around the throat until he could feel his dick and shot.

"Yeah you fucker. Take that fuckin' cop dick, faggot. Suck my jizz down your cock-sucking throat."

O'Reilly shot load after load deep in the dick-licker's throat. Suit lay limp in his sling of jockstraps. Sperm seeped around his lips and bubbled out his nose. It dripped on the floor in long strands of cock glue.

"That was a good fuck." Wolfe declared and pulled his dick out of the well fucked hole. It dripped on the floor between his legs. He took his baton and shoved it up the ass of Suit and left it there.

"Just in case someone else needs to tighten up his ass-ring when they fuck him," he declared to the men waiting for a piece of tail.

O'Reilly pulled his thick cop-dick out of Suit's mouth and wiped off the un-cut meat on Suit's salon cut hair.

"He's a good a cocksucker as Father Flannigan but you don't have to pray to get a good nut from him," declared O'Reilly as he walked back to the bar.

Suit lay in the sling. Cum dripped around the baton stuck in his ass and he coughed up jizz that dripped from the side of his lips to the floor.

One of the dockworkers that waited patiently for O'Reilly to finish, walked over to Suit, pulled his pants down and mounted Suit's head. He used the slave's hair to pull the jock covered mouth deep in his ass, feeling the slimed tongue work his hot hole.

"Hey Jack! Fucker got a tongue like a god-damn lizard," he yelled at his friend rubbing the mound in his pants.

Jack walked over and looked down at Suit's blue eyes staring up from the balls and dick that covered his face. Suit's eyes looked over Jack whose chest was bare and had the body of a god.

"Lance, you fucker, let me stick my fuckin' dick in that mouth of his."

Lance pulled the lapping head off his ass and felt the tongue graze his nut-sack searching for something to lick.

Jack pulled out a big fucking cock, smooth, hairless and hard as a steel pipe. He shoved it in the jock covered mouth hole and felt the tongue work the head of his dick.

"Damn that's good," he announced.

"Hey buddy, take the other end, I was getting a good rimming here and there's not enough room for that fuck monster of yours and my ass."

Jack chuckled but before he pulled his dick out, he shoved it in as far as he could. He pulled out and walked to the other end of the sling. Lance went back to pulling Suit's mouth deep between the cheeks of his ass.

"Suck that hole ass-wipe. Suck it good, fucker. Yeah that's it. Get your fuckin' tongue up there. Yeah, shit yeah."

Jack looked at the tight little ass with the night stick stuck in it. The black wooden rod waved around with Lance maneuvering of Suit's head back and forth in his ass crack.

"If we put a flag on the end of that stick we could enter this ass-hole in a fourth of July parade," Jack said just before he pulled the stick out and shoved his salami in.

"I can't believe how tight he feels after that fucking he got from Wolfe."

Lance turned around, having his hole slobbered on and sucked. Without missing a stroke, he shoved his horse cock in the mouth hole of the jock.

"Fucker loves cock. Loves to be treated like shit. That's those corporate types for you. All balls in the boardroom and bitches for real men at night. Ain't that right pussy-mouth? That's what you are ain't it? A pussy-cunt whore at night."

All Suit could do was grunt with the mammoth dick shoved deep in his gullet. Jack was tapping the tied up balls with the night stick. He watched them as he batted them side to side while his dick fucked the hot hole.

"Jesus A Christ. I think the fucker came," Jack said.

The roped up jock that held Suits cock and balls was dripping from the jock pouch. The cock glue dribbled down the sides of the stretched package and around Jacks dick plunging in and out of the ass-hole.

"The mother-fucker came. Can you believe that! What a fuckin' cock hound."

Jack started to beat the balls with the stick and he noticed that each time the balls were smacked, Suit's ass-hole tightened on his cock.

"Shit that feels good. Every time this night stick smacks those nuts, this guy's butt-hole clamps down."

"No shit," Lance exclaimed. "Let me try that."

Lance pulled out and traded places with Jack who handed him the night stick. First Lance smacked the nuts with the stick and watched the sphincter pucker.

"God-damn if you ain't right. That fuckin' pucker of his just begs for it. Don't it?"

Jack shoved his slimed coated cock down in the mouth hole and pinched one of the nipples on Suit's chest.

"Like I told you, pussy through and through."

"I can see that," Lance said and shoved his cock in to the hilt."

"Go on. Beat his fuckin balls with the god-damn stick. The queer loves it."

Instead, Lance grabbed the tied up package and used it to shove his dick into the ass. With one hand he yanked the cock and balls back and forth to move the ass on his prick and with the other. He used the baton to smack Suit in the gut.

"Fuck, his fuckin mouth is just like his asshole. It clamps down on my fuckin cock just like it did in his cunt."

The men fucked Suit at each end. One slapped his face, tweaked his tits and the other fucked his ass, pulling on his nuts and banging on his gut with the baton. Sweat poured off of Suit as he worked the two cocks. The men went faster, trying to outpace the other. They sat up a rhythm. When Lance pulled on the nuts, driving his cock in the ass, Jack slapped Suits face as his cock was pulled off. Then Jack yanked the nut-sack the other way, pulling his dick from the hot ass and smack Suit's gut with the night stick while the slave's mouth devoured Lance's cock.

Suit's body was shaking and the timber that held the rope above creaked with the swaying body held in the jock made sling. Suit looked like he was going to pass out from the beating he was taking and the cocks that were driven in him at each end. When Jack began to cum, he grabbed the rope that held the balls and yanked it hard to shove the ass deep on his cock and held it there.

"Fuck. That feels good," he said as his cock erupted deep in Suit's guts.

When he finished, he let go of the rope and Suit swung back on the cock in his mouth. Jack took the baton and replaced it in the well fucked hole.

Lance grabbed the head and kept his cock buried in Suit's throat while he shot load after load. When he was finished, he pulled out and turned around to get a little tongue action going on his crack.

He lifted Suit's head hard with a yank on his hair and relished the feel of the hot slimy tongue in his butt.

"Eat my hole fucker. Eat it good."

The two men in the corner came over to the ass end of Suit. The one with nipple ring shoved his cock in after taking the baton out of the ass. His friend got behind him and shoved his dick up his friend's ass.

When Lance had a good rimming, he went to the bar for a drink. That allowed one of the marines at the mouth hole. He was already naked. Having lost at strip poker and decided his nuts needed a good cleaning. The big hairy orbs were shoved in and the marine's cock hung over the face of Suit who was now looking straight up the ass crack of the marine.

The marine loved the tea bagging. He would dip down so that Suit could suck in more of the ball bag and at the same time, his nose was closer to the marine's delicious crack. The hairs on the marine's ass brushed against the tip of Suit's nose and tickled him, causing him to sneeze and blow air into the crack of the marine.

"Fuck that feels good," The marine said grinding his nuts into the mouth of Suit and making him sneeze again.

"If the fucker had another mouth, I'd shoved my ass crack in it right now," the marine said and began to jack his cock while his nuts were being sucked on, and Suit sneezing in his crack on occasion.

The two men at Suit's ass changed places, only the one fucking Suit had the baton in along side his dick and he was rubbing the tied up package of Suit's strung up cock and balls. The guy would rub them hard and then smack them, making the stick in the ass bounce and smack the two men daisy chained behind the ass.

The marine with his nuts in Suit's mouth started to cum and as he bellowed out, jizz flew and hit the two guys fucking. They shot, one in Suit's ass and the other in the ass of his friend. Once they came, the marine turned around to get his butt sucked. The two guys at Suits ass stuck the baton back in the butt and started to tweak Suit's nips and yank on his balls, when a very large dockworker started to shove the baton in and out of Suit's ass-hole.

"What a fuckin' scum bucket this piece of shit is," he said as he pushed the night stick deep into the butt and back out. He took his cock out and pissed on Suit, waving his dick and wetting Suit all over his body. The marine had a smile with Suit's tongue deep in his crack and his thighs clenched tight on each side of Suit's face.

"Sweet," said the marine as he bent over a bit more to get Suit's tongue further inside his butt-hole.

"This mother-fucker is a real fuckin toilet mouth ain't he," he said as sweat dripped down his back and into the crack of his ass where Suit's tongue lapped every drop.

Another marine came over and pulled the night stick out and shoved his cock in, fucking Suit hard and fast before he nutted. When he did, he took the baton, shoved it in the ass and reamed it good before taking it out. The slimed up end full of milky cock-snot dripped down the handle and the marine quickly shoved it in Suit's face rubbing the jock covered mouth where the tongue was embedded in the other marine's ass. Suit lapped at both with relish.

Men were lined up waiting to fuck the strung up ass or shoved their dick in the jock covered mouth. Some decided to beat his ass or tweak his tits. Others batted the jock covered cock and balls strung up high while Suit groaned and whimpered in delight. All the while, Wolfe and O'Reilly yelled out comments on how to treat the slut in the sling. Offered ideas and cheered the men on in their sexual frenzy.

Finally, as fewer men wanted to fuck the slut's cum filled ass or stick their dick in a mouth oozing with piss and semen, Wolfe walked over and stared down at Suits upturned face and spit on him right between the eyes.

"Look at yourself, you fucking pig. No one wants to fuck you anymore. You are so disgusting. You're trash. You're a cum-bucket. A filthy pile of cum encrusted jock and stink." Wolfe spat on him again.

The cop stood to one side of Suit, bent down and whispered in his ear.

"You need a shower, shit-for-brains."

He took the jock off of Suit's face, wadded it up and shoved it in Suit's mouth.

Wolf stared at the upside down eyes. "Eat it."

Suit gobbled at the jock. He chewed quickly and swallowed hard. His throat, now stretched, resembled a python swallowing prey.

Wolfe walked to the trussed up slave's side and un-tied the key knot. Suit's head and shoulders hit to the floor with a thud. The cock and balls, tied in the jock, stretched from the groin. His legs and sex still tied from the beam. A groan came from the floor where Suit's mouth dripped cock juice and phlegm from all the pricks, piss and jocks shoved in it.

Wolfe slowly walked back around Suit's head, stopping for a moment to shove his leathered boot top into Suit's mouth for a tongue cleaning. He lit a cigarette and watched the smoke curl before he threw the lit match on Suit.

A pitiful cry came from the slave, his tongue working feverishly on the leather, muffled the cry's tormented edge.

Wolfe walked around with a slow, deliberate step to the feet and legs hanging in the air. He took a drag off the cigarette and watched it meld with the vapor of men-smells. The cop removed the cigarette, reached over and snuffed it out in Suit's ass crack. All the slime in his butt sniffed it out, but the heat woke Suit up enough to bone.

Wolfe pulled the key knot on the legs and they dropped partially, the cock and balls stretched like a bungee cord. Suit looked imploringly at Wolfe, who smiled when he saw Suit's blue eyes stare at him.

Wolfe lifted the rope slightly and let go, it made Suit groan. "I should leave you like this, hanging by the balls. It would do you good."

Sweat poured from Suit's brow. His face flush, he hung there with the back of his head and shoulders touching the floor, the rest of him suspended by his nuts.

Wolfe grabbed the key knot and pulled. Suit crashed to the floor with a thud and immediately doubled up and grabbed his distended balls.

Wolfe kicked him. "Stop playing with yourself, you fuckin' fairy."

Another groan emitted from Suit. He forced his hands away from his still tied up cock and balls.

"Stand up worm."

The slave got to his knees and with some effort stood. Wolfe towered over him, spit on his face and then yanked the rope from his genitals.

The jock fell to the side. Suit's cock laid along his thigh, his balls dropped between his legs, descended a good eight inches from the crotch and his prick burped the pent up jizz that could now flow.

"You're a fuckin' mess. Get in the head and lay in the urinal until you're clean meathead."

Wolfe kicked him to send him on his way. Suit scrambled to the bathroom, when he got there, he lay in the urinal trough. Piss and cigarette butts coated the stained porcelain bottom.

Wolfe motioned for O'Reilly to join him in the can. The cop at the bar downed his scotch and followed.

A dim, naked light bulb in the middle of the room bathed the urinal and shitters with a reddish glow. The shitters had no privacy, three on one wall of the gray tiled room. In the middle of the floor was a drain. Next to a broken mirror on the wall was a rubber hose attached to a spigot, the end dripped water on the floor that followed the contours to the drain. One man was fucking another in the ass against the wall. He pounded the guy's butt as he licked the ear.

O'Reilly joined Wolfe at the trough, reached in Wolfe's leather jacket and felt his chest. They looked at each other long enough to size up their massive bodies of muscle.

O'Reilly shoved his tongue in Wolfe's mouth and held the cop's head in a long, hard embrace as their tongues fought one another.

Suit boned in the trough looked up at them. He stared at the muscled gods in their embraced. Their spit shined boots, by his spit, glistened in the haze of the red light. He wanted to tweak his nipples and jack his dick but knew better than to touch himself. He knew because when he did, terrible things were done to him. He wanted to touch his sore dick so bad he shook his hips side to side to bang the dick's head against the edge of the urinal he laid in.

Wolfe moved his foot and stepped on the dick with the sole of his boot. Suit looked in horror as the foot pressed harder against his cock and the porcelain. The two cops stayed in their embrace, ignoring the pleading look in Suit's face. Wolfe shifted his weight on the foot that pressed on the cock.

The face on the slave turned to a grimace. He clenched his teeth, shook his head from side to side, his hands became fists that squeezed the blood from the fingers. Wolfe turned his foot slightly crushing the prick beneath it.

Suit let out a high pitch wail of anguish. Tears formed and fell from his eyes to no avail as Wolfe ground the dick under his foot like it was a cigarette butt.

The two cops standing over Suit broke their embrace and looked down at the wreathing slave at their feet.

"Fuckin' worm was beating his meat." Wolfe exclaimed and lifted his foot off the squished dick, then kicked him in the balls.

O'Reilly pulled out his hose of a cock and started to piss all over Suit. Wolfe did the same, aiming some in the slave's mouth and his blue and purple prick. When they were through, they both took turns kicking him for a while when some marines from the bar came in.

"What the fuck?" said one of them.

"Dick breath here needs a bath. Stinks worse than a backed-up shitter," exclaimed Wolfe.

"Well I have to piss like a horse," said the other.

"Go ahead, the prick here loves it," said O'Reilly.

The two marines joined the cops, pulled out their cocks and hosed Suit down. He laid there being drenched in the piss of marines and cops. A smile crept across his face and his sore, bruised dick began to harden again.

One of the marines spit on his face while he played his stream across Suit's mouth. The slave swallowed then burped.

"Fuckin' pig," one of the marines said and kicked him before he shook his dick and walked out.

The other marine did the same soon after, and then left O'Reilly and Wolfe to Suit who walked out as well after they shook their dicks and hawked up a wad of spit on Suit.

He laid there in the trough, drenched in piss, spit and the small amount of water that dripped down the side of the urinal's walls. Left alone, naked and sore he waited for more men to come in. The two men fucking against the wall stopped when one of them saw the cops leave. They walked over to where the slave was in the urinal and ordered him to kneel. Suit got to his knees and the guy that was getting fucked earlier, stuck his dick in Suit's mouth. His partner went back to fucking his hot hard ass. Every time he pushed his dick in his friend's ass, the friend's cock was shoved down Suit's throat. It didn't look like they were ready to cum, enjoying their fuck and with the willing mouth on the guy's dick getting fuck. It was just too good to end.

Suit sucked the dick like a champ. His thin white body was covered in pubic hairs, cigarette butts, piss and spit from the urinal. His skin had a sheen to it that reeked of sex. His mouth worked the cock like the pro he was at sucking cock. He didn't miss a beat, and had the guy on the edge in no time.

"Shit Hank, this fucker has me ready to blow."

"Pull out and shove your nuts in his mouth. I ain't done fucking you yet."

That's just what he did. Grabbing Suit by the hair, he yanked him off his cock with a plop and before Suit could attach himself to the hard prick again, shoved his swollen nuts in the slave's mouth.

Suit worked them just as well. His well stretched out mouth could take a fire hydrant if he had to and the balls went in with a plop. Suits cheeks swelled out as he sucked and lathered the nuts with his tongue. He tried to get them down his throat by swallowing them. As each nut sucked into his throat, the ball-sack tightened.

"Fuck Hank, that fucker swallowed my god-damn balls." He said as he grabbed his cock and tried to hold back a volley of cock-glue that smacked against the side of the urinal just above Suit's head.

The next wad went straight up in the air and fell down over Suit's head and face, smacking with plops of creamed jizz.

"I couldn't hold back Hank. The fucker made me nut."

"Well I ain't through fucking you yet," he said and slammed his salami in hard. "I'm just going to have to keep fuckin' ya, Miller."

Another wad shot when Hank shoved his cock in deep and hard. The gob hit Suit right in the eyes. It smeared down his face and the nut-sack in his mouth.

Miller grabbed his balls and yanked them out of Suit's mouth.

"Damn, that's some suction you got going fucker."

Miller took his dick and smeared it up with the jizz on Suit's face. Once the cock was coated with goo, he shoved the slimed up dick-meat all the way down Suit's throat in one long lunge.

"Yeah! Fucker's got a throat like a cunt, only tighter."

Miller ground his groin in Suit's face. He pressed so hard that the back of the slave's head squished into the sticky goo Miller had shot on the urinal.

"I'm fuckin' loving it," Miller said and pressed hard on the cock in his ass. "Fuck me Hank. Shit, Jesus fucking Christ—fuck me."

Miller spread his legs as wide as he could. Hank's balls swung back and forth. The nuts banged on the back of his ass and when they swung forward, slammed Suit's chin, his mouth busy on the cock in it. Suit wanted to grab the balls and feel them, hoping they would be his next play toy.

"Oh fuck yeah, fuckin' hot ass," Hank said.

Suit could feel the dick in Miller's ass. He could feel it pressed deep inside when his lips were ground into the pubic hair surrounding the hot cock.

Suit could no longer resist. When Hank's nuts swung again and hit his chin, he reached up and took hold of them. They were big, hot and heavy. It was all he could do to keep them in one hand before he got his other one on them.

Suit's feet were planted on each side of his haunches. His asshole squatted over the urinal's drain acting like a plug. His battered and bruised cock was boned and sticking straight up. His balls nestled in the trough with the piss, cigarette butts, pubic hairs and spit. Suit was in heaven.

Some guys from the bar came in and went to the urinal surrounding the men busy fucking. They reached out and felt the hard ridges of the muscled bodies. Felt the hot sweat that glistened on their flesh.

Suit played with the balls in his hand. Miller now was fucking Suit's face while Hank fucked his ass. One of the guys standing next to Miller began to tweak his nubs and talk dirty in his ear.

"Yeah, fucker. Slam that dick in the cock-sucker's throat. Yeah fucker. Hot fuckin' dick. Throat fucking that ass-licker. You like it? Like having your cock in his hot mouth?"

Miller licked the man's face, licked the shadow of beard that bristled on his cheeks.

"You like getting fuck? Like having Hank's big ole' cock up your ass? I bet you do huh? Bet you like getting fucked real good. Like your titties played with too huh? Like having me tweak these pretty little nubs of yours. They look like tiny pricks don't they. Hot fucking stud with trained nips that get boned for dick."

A shiver went through Miller's body. He almost purred when he rubbed up the side of the man whispering what a slut he was in his ear.

Suit rolled the balls in his hands, it drove Hank crazy and he fucked harder and faster as someone behind him played with his ass.

"Fuck, I'm going to shoot!" Hank yelled out as he rabbit fucked Miller's ass.

The guy behind Hank had two fingers in his ass when Hank shot into Miller's butt. Miller shot again in Suit's mouth. It ran out over his lips suctioned on the cock.

"Fuck, that was good," Miller said as he pulled out his cock and wiped it on Suit's hair.

Hank and Miller stumbled out to sit at a table and left Suit to the group of guys waiting behind.

Suit looked up at them as he stayed in a squat, his ass covering the drain. Three of the men pulled their cocks out and began to piss on the slave, who gulped at whatever stream was near. The other two men pulled their dicks out and took turns shoving them in Suit's mouth. One of them started to piss and the other was slapping Suit's face before he shoved his dick in the mouth. The urinal was filling up. The trough was almost full of warm piss. Suit began to pee as well. It went straight up in the air and splattered on his belly before it dripped off his body and into the trough.

The two men taking turns fucking his mouth were banging away at his lips. Sometimes both of their cocks made it into Suit's mouth making the slave's cheeks bulge out.

At one point, one of them turned around and ground his ass in Suit's face as the others pissed in the guy's ass crack to watch Suit lap at the butt and the piss at the same time.

Another guy took his leather belt off and doubled it up. He began to beat Suit's chest, his tits and on occasion a blow would hit Suit's rigid cock.

The slut's chest began to glow from the smacking of the belt. The nubs of his nipples hardened and pointed out with the slap of the belt across them. Suit was pushed down in the trough and told to bath in all the piss and cum at the bottom. He rolled in it as the belt struck him on the back and ass. When he moved, the belt followed and smacked his tender balls, the side of his legs, his gut, everywhere Suit was exposed to the belt. His body, wet from the contents of the urinal took on a pink glow from the use of the leather until one of the men pulled Suit out of the urinal by his hair. He dragged him to the center of the room and forced him to lie on the cold tile floor.

With Suit's face up, he stared up at the hairy ass descending on him. Its hard melon globes spread to reveal a pink hole aimed for Suit's mouth.

The slave readied with his tongue out to penetrate the sphincter. As his eyes crossed to focus on the rosebud, he could feel the heat of the muscled butt just before it landed on his face.

His tongue penetrated the hot hole and Suit went to work with two hundred pounds of muscle sitting on his face, his tongue deep in the hole.

"Yeah, eat me fucker. Eat me good," said the man that squatted on his face.

Suit's eyes stared up at the butt crack and curve of the man's spine. The muscled back with the spine running to his ass crack acted like a furrow for all the sweat pouring from the stud, right into Suit's face. He could taste the musky ass, the stringent sweat and feel the hard flesh of solid butt cheeks.

The man began to squirm on the face. His ass ground on the tongue and he worked his crack up and down the slave's nose, mouth and lips.

The man on Suit's face reached over and lifted the slut's legs up and held them as another guy pulled out his cock and shoved it up Suit's ass for a good fucking.

Once he set up a rhythm of long dick strokes in and out of the small little butt, his cock became rock hard. The man leaned over to French kiss the guy on Suit's face and another dock worker got behind him with a big fucking dick and started to penetrate Suit's well stuffed hole.

Suit groaned as he felt his ass stuffed with two huge cocks, but nobody heard it. The ass on his face muffled the groan.

Suit felt the man on his face spread his legs further apart, allowing the two cocks in his ass better access. He felt like the wishbone of a chicken about to break in half as the pounding in his butt intensified. Both cocks lunged in and out of his ass at the same time. The guy on his face could see the cocks in Suit's gut swell when the pricks were pushed in and slacked when they pulled out near the opening. The two worked as a unit battering the butt-hole and forced Suit to dig even deeper in the ass on his face to suppress the pain from his butt-lips stretched to their limit.

Two men that stood nearby waiting their turn, started to kiss and feel each other bodies. They looked down at Suit and wanted to feel their cocks in his ass too, their butts on his face.

Deciding that they couldn't wait much longer, they both got in the middle of the orgy standing like bookends, their legs on each side of Suit. One put his cock in the mouth of the guy mounted on Suit's face. The other, with his back to his partner, put his in the mouth of the first guy fucking Suit's ass.

Two cocks were in the slave's ass, one guy on his face and two others getting a blowjob standing over Suit's body with their butts grinding against each other.

"Fuck yeah," said the guy with his cock getting sucked from the guy fucking Suit's butt.

"Hot fucking scene man," said his buddy as they both got blowjobs from the men in heat.

The guy sitting on Suit's face gave the legs he was holding to the guy fucking his face. Then he pulled up off of Suit's head and shoved his cock down the slave's throat. Suit's eyes were now covered by the man's balls as he sucked the fuck-stick in his throat.

A marine got behind the guy with his dick in Suit's mouth and shoved his prick up the man's ass. Suit could feel the balls hit his head when he slammed into the ass above him.

It was hard now to see where Suit was in the mass of flesh that covered him. Two men fucking his ass, one in his mouth, two guys over him with their dicks in the mouths of the others and now another fucking the ass that he finished eating out.

Sweat dripped from the men deep in their orgy. They cussed like marines, cops and dockworkers, swearing about the hot muscled bodies that were being fucked or fucking. Other men came and felt the hard bodies of those on the outside of the orgy, hoping to get in on the steamy sex, their cocks rigid as they jacked them and sometimes shot on the entwined bodies. Cum, sweat and piss lubricated the men, and at the bottom of it all was Suit, drenched in the sex of hot muscled men above him.

The dick in his mouth was replaced by a bubble butt blond without a feather on his ass. His tight little butt-hole fit just right on Suit's mouth, the mound of his ass cheeks settled over Suit's face. The slave's tongue dove in and out of the butt like it was a honey pot and the blond loved it. He squirmed on Suit's face, grinding his ass on the tongue and lips that worshipped his hard, white bubble butt.

Suit knew he was preparing him for a good fucking. He could tell the ass on his face wanted more, couldn't get enough with its tight pink hole that opened and closed on his mouth like a clam.

The cocks in his ass slammed in hard and stayed, he could feel what felt like gallons of jizz shoot deep in his butt. Soon they were removed and he felt another cock easily slide in and not long after, he felt a hand slide in with it, grabbing the cock and jacking off inside his guts. It felt like two cocks again with the fist and cock both up his ass.

The room grew hot and steamy as a Turkish sauna. Suit had more dicks stuck in his ass and mouth. He felt the slick goo of sex drop on him from above and the stink of men at play filled his nostrils.

When the men were done with him, he was left on the tiled floor of the tearoom with his tongue sticking out waiting for another ass. His butt-hole seeped jizz and piss and his body was slick with the sex of men. He yearned for another cock up his ass or in his mouth and when he looked around the room, most of the men had left to have a drink or play another round of cards. His eyes, covered in spit and gobs of cum, tried to focus. So, he swiped at them with his hand and when he looked again, there were two large dark shapes standing above him.

"Would you look at that," O'Reilly said.

Wolfe kicked Suit in the balls. "Leave this ass-hole alone for a second and he can't control himself."

The leathered cop grabbed Suit by the hair and dragged him back to the urinal. He pushed Suit's face in the trough. Then he dragged the slave's head back and forth in the bottom of the trough by Suit's hair.

"You fucking cum-bucket. I told you to clean yourself up. And what did you do?"

Wolfe yanked his head up by the hair and spit on his face. "You fucking whore. You've been letting every guy in the joint fuck you!"

Wolfe slammed his face back down in the urinal and rubbed it across the clogged drain before he yanked him up again by his hair. Suit came up sputtering, a mashed cigarette butt stuck on his cheek and pubic hairs on his lips.

"You fucking piece of shit! What are we going to do with you? You're filthier now then when we left you."

Suit looked down, his cock was hard, his ass dripped semen and before he could say he was sorry, he burped up jizz from his gut.

"Fuck! You're a god-damn sewer. You fucking piece of shit." Wolfe then kicked Suit in the balls.

The slave groaned, drew his legs up and looked at Wolfe's crotch. He wanted to suck the dick he could see through the leather. He could see the big un-cut meat pressed against the slick, black-hide of leather he licked, kissed and worshipped every chance he got.

O'Reilly grabbed Suit's jaw with his hand and forced him to look at the cop's face. He then spit in his face. It hit with a smack on Suit's nose, eyes and mouth. Suit reached with his tongue everywhere he could lap at the phlegm.

"He's fuckin' boned, Wolfe. Look at him. Sportin' his little thingy like it was a cock. Pathetic. He might as well been an alter boy for Father Flannigan. A little fairy for the good Fathers."

Wolfe screamed, "Get your fucking legs apart."

Suit spread his legs to get slammed by Wolfe's knee. - "Keep'em apart ass-hole."

The slave hung by his hair, his legs bent and apart as the leathered knee slammed into his balls.

Wolfe pushed him against the urinal, his head up against the rusty water that dripped down the yellowed sides and mixed with the piss. His knee slammed again and again into Suit's nuts. The slave kept his legs apart and his dick hard with each hit to his swollen balls.

When Wolfe was through, he let go of Suit's hair and the slave collapsed in a heap at the bottom of the urinal. With his head in a pool of piss, he stuck his tongue out and lapped the foul water like a thirsty dog.

O'Reilly and Wolfe looked at the scrawny dog of a slave, pulled out their cocks and pissed. Suit could feel their hot stream hit his body, he could smell the rancid piss gush from the piss-slits of the hard-bodied cops standing at the urinal, their cocks in hand, hanging over the end of their thumbs with the heads drooping down to unload their yellow stream.

Suit stared up at the two and his cock shot a wad of jizz on the side of the urinal. Immediately, Suit scurried to lick the wad as it dripped down the side of the pisser.

Wolfe and O'Reilly helped him by aiming their piss stream at the wad of cum and the opened mouth lapping at the goo.

From outside the head, Bull yelled, "Hey, O'Reilly!"

"Yeah. What is it?"

"Madame Woo wants you to take down the sign over the bathroom door, 'Toilet backed up. Use the urinal'. She says she runs a clean joint and not even the whores are backed up."

"All right. I'll be out in a minute as soon as I tell this urinal to stop advertising and shove his god-damn sign up his ass."

"Did Suit do that?" Bull asked.

"He's all pissy now, Bull. You want me to clean him up?"

"Tell that fucker to stop clowning around and get back to work. Jesus, I can't serve a drink without that little prick running off to the can."

CHAPTER SIX

The sailor's mouth held tight to the base of Sarge's dick. His baby-blues looked up at Sarge's face to see if he was ready to blow another wad.

"I wanna feel you suckin' sailor."

Tim sucked, which was hard to do since his throat was stuffed full of marine cock. But he did his best and used his throat muscles to nurse the dick, like a snake trying to swallow its prey.

"Oh, yeah sailor, suck that fuckin' dick. Yeah baby, eat it good. Eat my dick, cock-sucker."

Sarge's legs stretched out and his head went back clenching the cigar in his mouth.

"Fuck yeah. Take my fuckin load cock-sucker. Take it."

Tim's throat was working fast trying to get another load of spooge down his gut. His cheeks filled out with the overflow and some of the creamy jizz started to leak from his lips that were unbelievably stretched around marine horse cock. As the spunk swelled out his stomach, adding to loads already in his gut, he was able to swallow what he had stored in his cheeks. And then slurp the leakage at his lips before the goo fell on Sarge's balls.

The marine sergeant drifted off for a moment, his legs relaxed while his fucking horse-hung dick began to soften enough for the sailor's stretched out lips to ease up somewhat.

Sarge's hand stroked the blond curly hair of the sailor while Tim's eyes watched Sarge smile.

"Fuck yeah boy, you fuckin' took that load real good."

Sarge smiled and smoked his cigar as he watched the sailor, who looked as happy as a trained puppy.

"I think it's time for you to entertain me. What do you think sailor? Think you can perform a trick or two?"

"Sure Sarge, I'd love it. What you want me to do?"

"I wanna see you suck your own dick for a change. Can you do that? Can you suck your own fuckin' dick?"

"I think so Sarge, I use to do it back home on the farm."

"I bet you did a lot of things back on that farm sailor. Okay let's see ya suck your own god-damn cock, fucker. Pull that love toy out of your cunt and put it on the table here."

Tim obediently grabbed the plug and pulled it out of his ass. The slick black rubber glistened in the red glow of the Chinese lantern. He placed it on the table next to Sarge. Then Tim moved a few feet away from Sarge and sat with his legs crossed on the floor. Sarge poured himself another whiskey and picked up his cigar from the ashtray. He took a puff on the end and let it out slowly, all the time keeping his eyes on the sailor.

Tim rolled on his back with his legs still crossed. With his hands, he took one of his legs and pulled it until the foot and ankle rested behind his head. Then he took the other leg and did the same, only this time it was a bit harder than the first leg. Now his hard cock was close to his face waving in the air, the piss-slit dripping clear cock nectar. Tim's naked little butt-hole was spread and exposed from his ass cheeks being separated by his wide stretched legs. It seemed to wink at Sarge, its little pink folds looking like a rosebud.

The sailor's eyes were focused on his prize, his cock stood erect in front of him. He leaned more, and with his arms, pressed his legs further back to bring his cock to his lips. He could feel the tender head brush against his lips and taste the clear nectar of his own dick juice that glistened on the red velvety cock-head in front of him.

"Let's see ya do it sailor. Suck your own dick. Get that mouth of yours down on that prick, cock-sucker."

Sarge took a sip of whiskey from his glass and a puff on his cigar, which he blew the smoke from toward Tim who had just grabbed the head of his own dick with his lips.

Tim's mouth slid over the head, he looked so happy, Sarge thought, sucking himself off in front of the marine.

As his lips slid down, the sailor's mouth formed around his cock, taking in more and sucking harder.

Now Tim had a rhythm going, each time he came up, and then back down, a little more of his cock was sucked into his mouth. His little pink hole enticed Sarge. Spread bare in front of the marine that sat in the sofa chair, Tim sucked his own cock in front of him. Sarge took his foot and played with the edge of the hole with his boot, pressing softly on it to watch it open and gapped for him. Sarge's dick began to harden again.

Tim was really into sucking himself now, He wanted more of the tasty treat and it felt so good to feel his lips and mouth on his cock. His balls, stretched by the metal weight of the tube that encased the sack, fell down next to Sarge's boot. Sarge began to bat the balls back and forth with his boot while Tim sucked his cock.

"God-damn sailor, you're making me horny as shit watching you suck your own cock. Look at those pretty balls of yours, you like your new toy sailor? Like the ball weight I put on you?"

Tim looked at Sarge. He still had his dick in his mouth and could feel Sarge's boot bat his nuts back and forth, his balls grazed the lips of his pucker and drove him crazy. He muffled approvingly to Sarge, unable to say anything else because he was sucking his own cock.

Sarge got an evil grin, took a hit off the stogie and put his boot on the nuts. With a shove, he pushed Tim's balls into his ass, half the ball weight went with it.

Now Tim went wild on his cock. Sarge pressed on his ass and the sailor sucked his own dick down further. Tim was clawing at his butt checks to force more of his own cock in his throat.

Sarge smiled. The sailor was working hard on his dick and Sarge started to rock Tim by pushing on the cylinder that held the balls in the sailor's ass. He rocked the navy man back and forth with the push of his booted foot.

"Yeah sailor, suck your cock. Suck sailor, you fuckin' dick-licker. You like that sailor, like chowing down on your own fuckin' dick?"

Sarge rocked him so hard Tim almost went over backward. "That's it sailor, get down on your fuckin' dick. Get that mother-fuckin cock of yours all the way in your cock-sucking mouth."

Tim worked his cock. He could feel the velvety flesh of his own dick slide down his cock-sucking throat. The few blond pubes around his dick began to tickle his nose. Then his lips grazed the base of his dick. It felt so good to Tim, so fucking hot to have his cock down his own throat to nurse on.

Sarge stopped rocking Tim and watched how the sailor stayed down on his own dick until the boy had to raise up for breath, like a sub at sea, only to dive again and swallow his entire cock.

"Shit sailor, you are one mother-fucking, cock-sucking, love puppy. I could take you on the road. Would you like that sailor? Like me to show off your skills. Have men watch you suck your own god-damn dick? Would you sailor, huh? Maybe drag you around on a leash. Park your sweet little butt on a platform and have you show them all the tricks I taught ya. Like that sailor? Like being my trained little fuck toy?"

Tim was ecstatic, his balls up his ass, his throat fucking his own dick. Sarge watching it all and loving what he did. The sailor shook. He groaned long and hard as his lips searched for more of his own cock. His dick discharged gobs of thick cum right down his gut.

"Fuck sailor, you're shootin' your load down your own cock-sucking throat!" Sarge took his glass of whiskey and downed it in one gulp.

Tim went wild, his moaning grew louder. He wanted more of his own cum, more of his dick in his mouth. He didn't want to let go, break the suck he had on his own cock. His lips held fast, his cheeks sunken from the suction. He shot more, and the head grew sensitive but Tim couldn't let go. His face grew red until Sarge told him to stop sucking himself.

Tim looked up from his cock. Sperm seeped down from his lips. His dick, red and swollen, lay against Tim's cheek. He saw Sarge's stern face and could now feel the weight of his balls and the steel that wrapped them in his ass.

"I'm going to have to show you some self control sailor. You know when to stop? Know when to let go of your own dick?" Sarge slowly moved his head from side to side. "I don't think you do sailor. The next time you do your little trick I'll have you stop now and then, maybe beg a little. Would you like that sailor? Like having to beg to suck your own god-damn dick?"

"It felt so good Sarge. I had my cock down my throat and it felt so good."

Sarge looked down at Tim and smiled.

"I know it did sailor. You got to suck your own dick and I can't think of anybody better myself, than you, the cock-sucker you are, to suck a dick real good."

"Thanks Sarge." Tim's smile beamed from his pretzel like contortion he was in.

"Now I want you push your nuts out of your ass and suck on them. Can you do that sailor? You sucked your own cock. Let's see if you can suck on your balls too."

"I'll try Sarge. I sure will."

"You don't try sailor. You fuckin' do or die. You got that sailor? You're a fuckin' god-damn navy-man sailor. You don't fuckin' try. Do it sailor. Suck your own god-damn nuts."

"Aye, aye Sarge."

"That-a-boy sailor, that's the kind of attitude I like to hear. Let's see you do it then. Suck your nuts."

Tim energetic face looked like he was being treated to a lollipop. "Sir. Yes sir."

Tim grunted, and his nuts, along with the metal cylinder, plopped out of his ass. He slid one hand down to where his nuts were hanging and grabbed the five inch cylinder that encased his ball-bag. He then raised them up and began to mouth the orbs at the bottom of the metal pipe. First one nut went in and then the other. Tim's nuts were stretched upward. His cock lay to the side, and thickened.

When Tim worked the other nut into his mouth he looked like a squirrel with cheeks stretched out and full.

"That's it sailor, suck on those balls of yours. Give 'em a good cleaning sailor. Put a shine to those nuts of yours."

Tim played his tongue over the smooth orbs. The feel of his own balls in his mouth was a thrill. The hard round egg shaped gonads excited the sailor so much his dick began to grow and harden again.

"Look at that sailor, you're fuckin' dick is boned again. You just filled up your gut with your own jizz and now your dick is boned. Shit sailor, you are one fuckin' horn dog."

Tim began to hum with his balls in his mouth. It was almost as good as having his cock in his mouth and he wondered if he could take his nuts with the cylinder down his throat too. He sucked harder on his nuts but the weight of the steel was heavy and his balls had been stretched. He tried to bend more but his back wouldn't give.

Sarge looked at the sailor's struggle to swallow his nuts like he did his cock. He picked up the butt-plug.

"I think you need some help sailor. I think you need an incentive to get those nuts of yours down your cock-sucking throat."

Sarge bent over and shoved the plug up Tim's ass. He held it there for a moment and then pulled the plug part way out before he shoved it back in. Sarge watched the sailor's ass-ring stretch around the widest part of the plug before he slammed it back in the hot hole of the sailor.

Tim loved it and he soon found he could apply more suction to his nuts. The cylinder began to disappear in his mouth. His balls began to slide down his throat.

"That's it sailor. Suck those fuckin' nuts of yours. Suck sailor. You fuckin' cock-sucking bitch. Suck!"

Sarge hammered Tim's butt-hole with the rubber plug. He shoved it in and out and at last, Tim had his nuts down his throat along with the metal pipe that stretched them.

"God-damn sailor, you've got your nuts down your cock-sucking throat."

Tim's prick was rock hard once again and leaking jizz juice.

"Okay sailor, get those fuckin' nuts out of your mouth. I need some attention here on my own god-damn ball bag."

Sarge yanked the plug out of Tim's butt and watched the sailor untwine himself.

Sarge poured whiskey into both glasses on the small table next to him and then placed his stogie in the ashtray.

"How would you like to sit on Sarge's lap?"

Tim shook his head affirmative.

"Come up here and shove my baby-maker in your ass. Sarge is gonna play with your titties for awhile."

Tim's eyes widened at the news. He stood up and stretched. The sailor tightened his gluts and flexed his arms, putting on a show for Sarge. His nuts hung down, his cock stood rigid and goo spit from its end. Tim turned and showed his ass lips stretched and puffy for big cock.

Sarge placed the butt plug on the table as Tim climbed up on Sarge's lap and grabbed the marine's cock, stuffing it up his loose ass before he settled down, his back on Sarge's chest. The giant cock stuffed his ass. Tim's ball sack, incased in the steel pipe, pulled down to the edge of the cushion.

Tim laid his head against Sarge's chest. He felt the curly hairs on his cheek. The marine handed him his drink, and then Sarge picked up the other one to sip himself.

"Yeah, you fuckin' hot mother-fucker. You like Sarge's pussy-banger. Don't you cock-sucker."

Tim murmured approvingly while Sarge's hand felt for the rubbery nub of his nipple.

The marine took a sip of whiskey before he said, "Yeah, Sarge's is gonna get you good and fucked before you go back to your shipmates."

Sarge's fingers rolled the nipple back and forth while Tim groaned and wreathed, his cock hard and leaking fuck juice. He squirmed on the dick deep in his guts.

Sarge took another sip of whiskey before he grabbed the sailor's cock and milked it for some goo, bringing the cock-snot up to the sailor's mouth for him to lick off his hand. Sarge's other hand played with the nipple, flicking it back and forth. Tim groaned as his tongue lapped the hand presented to him and when he finished licking the goo, Sarge picked up Tim's glass and gave him a drink of whiskey.

"Fuck Sarge, that feels so fuckin' good."

"You like that sailor? Like having your titties played with? You like that?"

"Yeah Sarge. I like it a lot."

"Your nipples look like tiny cocks sailor. You play with your nipples? Do ya?" he asked while he flicked one nub and then the other.

"Yeah Sarge, I do. I'm always horny. I wake up horny."

"I can tell. Your dick is always hard. Fuckin' slut. You a fuckin slut? Are ya? A cock sucking, mother-fucking slut? Are ya sailor?"

Sarge dipped his fingers in whiskey and shoved them in Tim's mouth. The sailor gurgled around the fingers, covering them in spit. Sarge went back for more cock-slime, milking the sailor's cock. He brought back four fingers covered in cock-goo and stuck them in the sailor's mouth as if it was his ass. The marine's cock hardened more and stretched the sailor's asshole. Standing up while Tim was still impaled on the marine's dick, the sergeant grabbed his nipples and cock-walked the sailor around the room bouncing him on his fuck-stick. Tim's weighted nuts swung in the air. The ball stretcher had pulled them halfway to his knees. When Sarge got to the back of the chair, he shoved Tim over it and started to slam his cock in and out of sailor's gaping hole.

"Mother-fucking cunt. Shit, you make me so fuckin' horny. You goddamn fuckin' slut," Sarge yelled with each thrust deep in the sailor's ass.

Tim's balls banged on the back of the chair with a grunt squeezed out of his lungs with each thrust.

Sarge slapped his ass with the palm of his hand, "Tighten that hole up sailor."

"Yes sir!"

Another slap rang out and another, "Get that mother-fuckin cunt of yours tight sailor."

"Yes sir," Tim yelled with each slap of Sarge's hand.

The marine slammed the sailor's ass over and over. The chair was moving across the room, pass the table it was next to with Sarge piston fucking the sailor with his big fat fucking dick.

When the chair hit the side of the bed, Sarge laid into Tim's ass, pressing the cheeks of his butt until the hole was flat against the base of Sarge's pubes.

The marine blasted another load deep in the sailor. It oozed out around where his cock was buried in Tim's ass.

"Shit sailor, you took my fuckin' nut again," he said while pulling the pussy-ripper out of Tim's butt. The ass-lips clung to the last moment as the donkey dick withdrew from the sailor's bowels.

Once the cock came out, Sarge reached between the sailor's legs and grabbed his weighted nuts. Without hesitating, he shoved the balls, stainless steel stretcher and all, up the sailor's ass. Then Sarge walked back to where the butt-plug sat and brought that back. He placed the cone on the butt lips of the sailor's hole and shoved. Now the sailor had his nuts, the metal weight and the plug imbedded up his ass.

"Clean my fuckin' dick, sailor," Sarge commanded.

Tim turned around and knelt at Sarge's feet. His lips went out to the slicked up cock and he began to lap the fuck-stick. He first licked off the jizz that still flowed from Sarge's piss-slit. Then he licked the slicked sides before he started on the base of the cock and the balls.

Sarge's balls were big and heavy. They smelled and tasted of sex. And Tim's tongue lapped at them, running his mouth over every groove and crevice before he swallowed one-and then the other nut.

He hung from Sarge's balls. His mouth bulged with cheeks full of nut-sack.

"Suck those balls sailor. Suck-em good cock-sucker. Yeah, that's it baby. You getting Sarge all boned up again."

The sailor massaged the balls in his mouth with his tongue and lips, before he pulled off them with a plop.

"Let me suck your cock Sarge. Please let me. I'll suck it good."

"Okay sailor, you go ahead and nurse that baby maker for me. Sarge is gonna get you ready for the boys downstairs."

The sailor grabbed the marine's cock with both hands and attached his mouth to the end, nursing it like a baby on a bottle.

"Yeah, that's it sailor. Suck my fuckin' dick. Suck it boy. Get me good and hot, fucker."

Tim worked the cock like the valiant cocksucker he was. He forced fed his self all the dick he could. Gorging on dick meat, he worked Sarge's glue gun with all the cock-snot he could swallow. Sarge slapped the sailor's ass, turning the ass a bright pink and then red. Once the butt was nice and tender Sarge took the shoelace he used to pull the sailor's nuts through the steel weight and tied it to the flange of the butt-plug. He took the other end and tied them to where the balls were shoved up the sailor's ass.

After a few more smacks to Tim's ass, Sarge pulled the plug out of the sailors butt and watched it fall with the ball weight just short of hitting the floor. The sailor groaned and sucked harder as the plug swung back and forth pulling the nut-sack further down.

Sarge pulled the sailor off his dick with the sailor's lips trying to cling to the cock.

"Stand up sailor and spreadem'".

Tim stood straight with his legs spread and the plug swinging beneath his balls.

"I think we need a bit more length. Get me the other shoelace sailor."

Tim rushed to where his shoes were and unlaced the other shoe, bringing it back to Sarge. The marine untied the shoelace from the sailor's nuts and tied it to the other shoelace to double the length. Then he re-tied the butt-plug with the shoelaces back to the sailor's nuts, just below the steel weight. The plug now hung just an inch or so from the floor between Tim's legs.

"Swing-em sailor," Sarge barked.

Tim began to move his hips back and forth, with his nuts straining with the added weight of the butt-plug. Each swing brought the plug higher in front and behind Tim, until the plug was nearing Tim's face.

"Catch that plug with your mouth sailor."

Tim reached out with his open mouth to grab the prize as it swung up, but missed, sending the plug straight down and bouncing on the floor, stretching the sailor's nuts further and making Tim bend his knees with the added stress.

Sarge screamed into Tim's ear, "Straighten those fuckin' legs sailor, or I'll add your shoes to them."

"Yes sir. Will do sir."

Tim tried again, tried to grab the plug but missed, but this time when the plug fell, he kept his legs straight and only groaned when the plug hit the floor and bounced, stretching his balls almost to his knees.

"Again sailor."

Tim rotated his hips back and forth and watched the heavy plug swing up and closer to his mouth. Once the plug was high enough, he strained his neck and clamped on the butt-plug, holding it in his mouth.

"That-a boy sailor. Now do it again."

Tim beamed in pride and spit the plug out. He started to swing his nuts once more until the plug was high enough to catch in his mouth. This time it was perfect.

"Wait till the boys see your new trick. Shove that plug up your ass sailor, we'll go downstairs and show you off."

Tim pulled the plug from his mouth and shoved it up his ass. His nuts were stretched with the weighted steel and slapped against his thighs with each step. Sarge held the door for him and the sailor proudly walked out with Sarge behind slapping his butt to hurry him down the hall and stairs.

CHAPTER SEVEN

At the bar, Suit was now naked except for his necktie, which was hung around his neck like a noose. Kneeling beside the poker table, one of his polished loafers was shoved halfway up his ass. He was busy giving a spit shine to the boots of a marine at the poker table. Suit's tongue lapped at the polished toe, his lips and mouth black with shoe polish.

Sarge walked over to the bar top and pulled out two stools. "Get up there sailor,"

Tim climbed on the stools putting one foot on each. His legs were now spread and as soon as he was in position, Sarge yanked the plug from his ass and let it fall. The sailor kept his legs straight and when the weighted plug dropped its accorded length he let out a grunt.

"Okay boys. Anyone want to place a bet that Sailor Boy can catch the butt-plug in his mouth?"

One of the dockhands yelled out, "We all know you've been training him to catch it Sarge!"

A general agreement came, along with a laugh, from everyone in the bar. Even Madam Woo, perched on her barstool near the door with her cigarette placed in its long ebony holder, cackled.

"Okay. Tell ya what, you sea dogs. We'll blindfold him. How about that!"

There was a murmur all around before Bull slammed down a ten. "You're on Sarge, but first let's give that sailor a shot of rye. He looks like he could use it."

Others started to place bets and one of the marines grabbed Suit by the tie, spit in his face and yanked the tie off his neck. Suit went back to polishing as soon as he saw he was no further use to the marine.

With tie in hand, the marine walked over to the sailor and told him to squat so he could blindfold him. Once the tie was secured he took the filled to the rim whiskey shot, and had the sailor slug it down. With a tug on the sailor's nuts, he told him to stand straight and start swinging.

The sailor, a little unsteady, but use to a ship's roll, began to swing the plug between his legs. The drill instructor looked at the pile of cash he could loose.

"I'm counting on ya' sailor," Sarge yelled in encouragement.

Even Madame Woo placed a ten spot on the bar.

The plug swung between the sailor's legs, with each pelvic thrust Tim made. Each swing brought the plug higher, and when Tim felt the rubber dick hit his back between the shoulder blades he knew it was high enough to catch. On the next swing, he gave a quick pelvic fuck motion and opened his mouth as wide as he could.

The plug landed with a plop in the sailor's mouth. Sarge stood there beaming with pride at his Sailor Boy. Madame Woo's eyes rolled to the ceiling before she took a long drag on the ebony cigarette holder. The boys at the poker table mumbled, saying, "Why the fuck didn't we train Suit to do something like that?"

Sarge looked around at the disappointed crowd. "Well boys seeing what good losers ya' all are. Drinks are on me!"

That brought the house to cheers and Madame Woo smiled at the thought of getting her money back and then some. One of the marines kicked Suit in the nuts and told him to get his fuckin' face cleaned up. He was a mess.

As Suit stood up to go and wash, the marine took the shoe from his ass. Just as Suit got to the bar, he threw the shoe, smacking the back of Suit's head with it. That brought another round of laughter.

Sarge helped Tim down from the bar stools and took the blindfold off. "Ya did good sailor. What can I give you for makin' Sarge proud of ya?"

"Fuck me Sarge. Please? Let me suck your cock. Okay?"

"Shit sailor, I'll do one better than that. I'll let the whole damn bar fuck ya'. How about that!"

The sailor's smile said everything.

Sarge grabbed Tim by the shoestring hanging from his balls. He took him over to a card table and had the sailor lay on his back. Tim's head hung over one end and his ass over the other.

The marine asked Bull to get him the rope from behind the bar. After he removed the shoestring, he tied the sailor's nuts with the hemp rope. Then he pulled on Tim's ball sack, making sure they were secure. The sergeant then looped the thick rope around the sailor's chest so that his pecs popped out and the nipples stood up real perky. With the rope secured around each ankle and tightened, the sailor's legs rose in the air spread-eagled. He finished with securing the nuts to the end of the rope so they were taught to grab onto when rutting that fine bubble ass. Tim's man-cunt stretched open. The sailor's hot pink hole winked at the crowd.

Sarge yelled out with a yank on Tim's balls making sure everything held. "There he is men, legs to Jesus. Prime navy ass waiting for all the cock it can get."

The sailor's ass spread opened so that the pucker looked like the bull's eye on a target. His mouth hung over the end of the table with drool dripping from the corner, waiting to be filled with hot, hard cock.

The men gathered around Tim's stretched out body, they ran their hands over his muscled torso, tweaked his rubbery nipples and pumped his prick for cock goo to finger fuck his mouth and ass. With Suit's mouth cleaned off, Bull ordered him to lick the sailor's ass well and keep it primed. Suit knelt at the table and shoved his face into the hard ass cheeks, tongue fucking the sailor until his spit ran down the sides of his face.

One big marine smacked Suit on the back of the head, then grabbed Suit by the hair and pulled him off the ass, it made a sucking noise when his lips were disengaged from the sailor's butt-hole. The marine then shoved Suit's mouth on his mammoth cock, skull fucking him until he chocked and gagged, bringing up phlegm that covered the ten-inch prick, round as a stove pipe. Then the marine, in one shove up the sailor's ass, crammed his thick barracuda all the way to the pubes, pulling on the rope tied to the sailor's balls to keep him from scooting forward off the spike deep in the sailor's gut. Suit got back to work, licking the giant prick as it went in and out of the ass. He licked at Tim's butt-lips and the marine's balls that smashed against his face.

One of the dockworkers, a big black stud, stood at the sailor's mouth teasing the navy man's lips with his anaconda of a cock. It hung out from his jeans, still soft and a good foot and half long. The head covered the sailor's mouth and Tim's tongue licked as best he could at the shiny ebony knob. When he shoved the snake-like cock in Tim's mouth and down the throat of the sailor, Tim's neck filled out and you could see the cock's head move down his gullet and back up. Tim's eyes were wild looking as the great nut sack of the dockworker smacked his face. The sailor's teary eyes glazed over in lust as the fuck stick skewered his mouth and throat, shoved deeper and harder down his throat.

Another dockworker, a big hairy Italian with a dick just as big, began to rub the piss slit of his cock over the stretched lips of the sailor, lubricating them with his cock juice while the ebony stud fucked the sailor's face.

"I'm a gonna fuck that mouth good," he said as he started to piss on the cock where it went in and out of the hot sailor's mouth. Suit heard the splash of piss on the floor and crawled under the table to lap up what fell. When the Italian was done pissing, the big black cock shot creamy-white dick glue. It seeped over Tim's lips as he pulled the prick from the sailor. Tim's tongue managed to grab some of fuck juice from the slick black cock before the Italian's salami was shoved in. Suit finished licking up the last of the piss and went back to lubricating Tim's ass-lips with his tongue when the next marine took over.

When the marine who had just fuck the hell out of Tim went to the bar for a drink, before getting back in line for another good fuck, he asked Bull, "Where in hell did you pick up Suit?"

Bull poured him a drink and then said, "Well I'll tell ya. About a year ago, it was kinda slow in here. Not much goin' on when that ass-hole over there," he pointed to Suit licking the butt of the guy now fucking Tim, "Came in dressed like some fucking rich prissy cock-sucker."

Bull looked over at Madam Woo who could hear him tell the story and she winked at him to go on. "Well he announced to Madam Woo, he was the new owner of this place and he wanted her out, and the bar closed. He had plans to make it an upscale drinking hole for rich bitches, shit like that."

The black dude came over and ordered whiskey up. Bull took out a fresh glass and filled it before he went on with the story.

"He was threatening Madam Woo and saying all kinds of shit. Like what a low life scum she was and only sewer rats would come to a dump like this. So I came around the bar while Madam Woo read the legal shit he gave her."

The ebony dockworker looked at the size of Bull, six foot six if he was an inch, and about two hundred and sixty pounds of solid muscle. "Shit, bet that put the fear of god in him," the dockworker said.

Bull smiled and said, "I looked in his fuckin' face and spit a loogie right between his eyes."

Madam Woo leaned closer and said, "Oh you should have seen pretty boy over there, he went white as ancestor ghost." She then flicked the end of her long ivory cigarette holder and when the ash fell to the floor, Suit scrambled over to lick it off the wood planks before going back to service the next marine's ass that was fucking Tim.

Bull had a broad smile as he wiped the counter top with Suit's dress shirt. "Then I held him up by his tie. The fucker's legs were dangling and flaying in the air. He gurgled and gagged, his prissy face turned blue and all contorted like. Then he pissed his pants so bad it ran on the floor."

I said to him, look you fuckin' piece of shit, I'm going to tear your fuckin' head off and use it to beat the living crap out of you if you ever fuckin' threaten Madam Woo again. Then I dropped him and rubbed his face in his own piss."

"Pretty boy wasn't so pretty then," Madam Woo interjected.

"When I was through cleaning the floor with his face, I kicked him right in the nuts three or four times. He moaned like a fuckin' whore getting stiffed for a blowjob. And when he turned over, I saw he had boned in his pants. That faggot loved everything I did to him."

Madam Woo inhaled on her cigarette holder and blew a smoke ring. "He so cheap, I have to give customer change for dollar when they pay for fucking his scrawny ass." She then chortled and flicked another ash to watch Suit run over again and lick it up. "I out of quarters now, so he has to blow them for quarter until I can give change for them to fuck him. He works at the end of the wharf, after closing. The winos and derelicts come to have some white-butt. They won't pay more than seventy-five cents to fuck him, a quarter for a blow. He so cheap, old Agnes one-tooth, with a hump, she live in dumpster. She won't fuck them for less than dollar. They like Suit better. Get change for cheap wine and their cocked cleaned off. Suit, he cheapest fuck around."

Bull then interjected, "That little bastard, kept whining he was sorry, his daddy gave him the place to get rid of him."

The marine asked, "His daddy?"

Bull answered, "Yeah. He's some rich ass son of some fuckin' millionaire and the old man caught him blowing the help at their mansion. The wimp asked me if we would hire him, he'd sign the deed over to Madame Woo. I told him though, if you fuckin' want to work here, I want you in a fresh suit when I open the place up. Every day at opening time, he's kneeling by the front door, bright as a daisy, dressed in some Armani outfit."

Another guy came over and told Bull the toilet was backed up.

"Kick that fucker sucking butt-hole in the nuts and tell him to get his ass in the head and it better sparkle."

The dockworker smiled, walked over to where Suit knelt behind a big hairy guy banging the sailor. Suit's tongue was rutting the stud's hairy ass, and landed a ball smashing kick right to Suit's nads. As he rolled on the floor grabbing his nuts in pain, the dockworker spat in his face and told him what Bull wanted him to do. Suit crawled toward the shitter on his hands and knees.

"I don't know how many of those damn fancy clothes he has left. But he comes here each day sporting a fresh new one, and by the time we close the bar, they're just a bunch of rags in the corner. We use them for cleaning up. So you know we got a class A joint here. It's cleaned by only the best clothes that ass-hole wears."

The men then turned and watched as Tim took another big cock, at both ends. Jizz was running from his ass and mouth and dripped in a pool to the floor waiting for Suit's return to lick it all up. Sarge was playing poker with some of the boys resting between fucks when they commented and thanked Sarge for letting them use the sailor.

"Yeah boys, best navy ass I ever ran into," said Sarge, "I'm gonna have a tattoo put on his butt, 'Property of U.S. Marines'. That will stir them up on board ship when he goes to take a shower."

"They'll fuck the livin' hell out of him Sarge." One of the men said.

"I know, he gets antsy before shore leave and that way I don't have to spend too much time getting him stretched out for this cunt ripper of mine," Sarge said, patting the bulge in his pants.

The cops came to the card table where Sarge was playing poker. The four of them gathered around the table with their batons in hand, slapping them on the palm of their other hand. It looked intimidating and some of the dockworkers nearby cleared away in case a fight broke out.

"O'Reilly patted Sarge on the shoulder with his night stick, "You boys aren't bettin' the family farm now are ya?"

Sarge acted like O'Reilly wasn't there and kept on playing.

He threw in more chips to the growing pile. "Wanna get in on the action, O'Reilly?"

"Gambling is against the law. Didn't you know that?"

Sarge threw down his cards, announcing he had a royal flush and took the pile of chips. "Who said we were playing for money, O'Reilly? All I see is chips."

"We know what happens at the end of the night with those chips sergeant. You boys cash them in. Don't ya?"

"Who says?"

"I say."

Sarge began to deal the cards out. "Well, I guess you're gonna have to wait until closing time to find out."

O'Reilly looked at the other three cops before he said, "Me and the boys don't have all night, but how about we bet these two rookie's to get in on the action."

Sarge looked at the two rookie cops. One was next to Wolfe and the other next to O'Reilly.

"I don't think their skinny asses could go ten minutes. How many chips do you want for them?"

The two younger officers looked at each other and at the size of Sarge. They knew how rough these men played and the two young cops began to sweat.

"Oh I say about a hundred in chips for each."

"Shit, a hundred each. O'Reilly if you loose your chips, well, I'm gonna get my two hundred worth out of these two if it takes all night."

"Well, a hundred for me and the other for Wolfe here. He'd like to get in on the action too."

"I see. And do these two agree to the deal?"

"Oh, I think they do." O'Reilly turned a stern eye toward the two rookies. "If they don't want to do graveyard on the eastside."

O'Reilly looked at one and then the other of the two rookies and asked, "Now what do ya say boys. You want ta' take a sportin' chance? Or you want ta' work the eastside until hell freezes over."

Without hesitating, the two young officers agreed to honor the bet.

"That settles it then."

"Pull up a chair, O'Reilly, you too Wolfe."

The two men pulled up chairs to the table and Sarge handed them each a hundred in chips.

The two cops were dealt cards and the play began with the two rookies looking over the shoulders of the cop they were standing next to.

One of the rookies looked across the room where Tim was servicing a couple of rough looking characters. The sailor had a dick up his ass and two guys taking turns in his mouth. Suit was on the ground sucking ass. The rookie cops had a delicate look with peach fuzz on their face and rosy cheeks, now flush. The dark haired rookie, next to Wolfe, felt his ass-hole pucker when he saw a Cajun dockworker slam the biggest dick he had ever seen up Tim's ass like he was laying pipe.

O'Reilly won the first hand and as he raked in the chips, chided Sarge, saying maybe he'd like to put the sailor's ass up for collateral if he lost his chips.

"The boys at the station could use a good piece of ass. I could tie him up in a cell and have him busy for a few days."

Sarge looked at O'Reilly straight in the eyes, "That sailor is marine property. He ain't goin' no where."

Wolfe chuckled and raised the bet of the play. "I have a special place in my cold fuckin' heart for sailors, sergeant. Why, he wouldn't be quite the same once I'm through with his ass."

Sarge chewed on his cigar and threw in more chips to the pile.

The two rookies were smiling, less nervous than before. Wolfe won the next round and the cards were shuffled and played out again. Sarge's pile of chips had thinned down.

Wolfe dealt the next hand as others gathered to see if Sarge would lose the sailor or win two hot cops.

The only noise in the room was at the table where Tim had a big marine plugging his ass. The guy's biceps popped out like cannon balls. Unshaved, he was taking his time fucking. One hand held a cigar and the other a beer. His arms were hairy and so was his chest, with a trail of dark hair riveting his abs. He had his shirt off, hat on and his cock and balls hanging out of his fly. Boots spit shined by Suit, his hard marine ass pumped slow and steady into Tim's creamy-white butt.

The sailor's mouth was full of a dockworker's nuts. An uncut cock was being jacked over Tim's chest and one of the guy's hands was tweaking Tim's tit, making his eyes flutter.

Each of the men picked up their cards. A bet was made, chips flew and the house knew that no one would fold on this hand. The ante was upped and Sarge's pile was down to two chips. He toyed with them, looked poker faced at the two cops and threw them into the pile.

"All or nothing," Sarge growled and threw down his cards.

Four pretty queens stared up with a Joker.

The others turned blank. The two young rookies thought the older officers were going to smile and display a better hand. They had stopped smiling, stopped snickering and their tight little assholes started twittering.

"Show-em and weep boys." Sarge said with a smile as he swept in the chips.

The two young rookies took a look at Sarge as the men around the table cheered, knowing what delights were in store for them.

Sarge yelled at the rookie cops. "Strip. Ya fuckin worms!"

The two rookies laid their hats on the table. Took their shoes off and undid their pants. With only boxers on, their sinewy bodies showed the hard training of the police academy.

When they stripped off their shorts the men cheered. Tight little hard asses and cocks, half hard, jutted out and curved. The nibs on their tits were swollen and puckered, looking for a good tweak.

"Look at that. Like two fuckin' Greek statues." Sarge licked his lips. "I don't know which one to fuck first."

The drill instructor squeezed the bulge in his pants real good as the two rookies admired how fast the sergeants fuck stick began to grow down his pant leg.

Sarge pointed to the redheaded rookie next to O'Reilly. "What's your name meat-head?"

"Sean, sir."

"And you dick-wad," he said to the other rookie.

"Bobby, sir."

"Okay ass-holes, and I really mean that. You, Sean bend over the table and spread them.

"Yes sir,"

"Bobby, you bend over next to him and get your butt as close to Sean as you can. I wanna dick both you cock-suckers."

The two naked rookies bent over the poker table as close to each other as they could get. Their cock and balls hung between their legs with their little tight butt-holes winking at the crowd.

"Suit! "Sarge yelled.

The slave came scrambling over and knelt in front of the sergeant. Sarge pulled out his salami and his bag of nuts, he held out his cock toward Suit.

"Get your fucking mouth slobbering on my dick, shit-for-brains."

Suit's mouth went to work faster than a ten dollar whore on the sergeant's cock. He licked at the sides and shoved his mouth over the head forcing it to the back of his throat. He coughed up slime and coated the sergeant's dick with a thick coat of mucus.

"Now get your nasty fucking mouth on the redhead's asshole, papa is coming home."

Suit turned to Sean and shoved his tongue up the rookie's butt. He licked all around the hole and slobbered in the crack.

"That's enough. I think he's enjoying it too much. Now get to work on the other hole."

As soon as Suit moved to the next butt, Sarge shoved his entire fourteen inches up Sean's ass in one stroke and ground his dick hard into the creamy ass cheeks of the rookie.

The cops face contorted. He bit his lower lip and held tight to the table, his knuckles turning white. Bobby, enjoying Suit's tongue working his hole, turned white when he saw his buddy's face.

"Shit Sean, you look like you've got a baseball bat up your ass."

Sean looked at Bobby and through clenched teeth said, "I do. And your next."

Bobby look of terror said everything. He clenched his sphincter down on Suits tongue causing the wet muscle to push out. Suit was a bit bewildered; everyone loves his tongue up their ass. He put his lips around the little butt-hole and sucked. When he had a good suction going he shoved his tongue back in and reamed the rookie with everything he had in him. The tight little hole started to relax.

Sarge pulled out and shoved Suit aside. He aimed his hard glistening dick and slammed the baby-maker home in Bobby's ass. The rookie's eyes crossed. His feet went up on his tip toes as he held tight to the table.

Sarge slammed that ass good and hard. He pulled out of the hole and slammed back in to the pubes, grinding his cock deep in the rookie's gut before taking it completely out and shoving it in again.

The table shook with the pounding. Men had to hold it in place to keep it from sliding across the room.

Sarge pulled out of Bobby and shoved it back in Sean's butt. The rookie held tight as the fucking began. As Sarge fucked, the rookie's face began to relax. Soon he had a smile on his face and pushed his white bubble ass back to meet the pounding. Sarge worked Sean's hole real good before he went back to Bobby's butt. Sean looked disappointed that his hole wasn't filled with hot hard cock.

Bobby's white knuckles began to relax too. He started to purr and drool began to form at the corner of his mouth. His small tight ass relaxed and he spread his legs a bit further to get more cock. The two rookies started to kiss each other. Their tongues dueled with each other as one was fucked and the other waited.

"Get Sailor Boy over here," Sarge announced.

The men fucking Tim untied him and set him free. He reported for duty, standing at attention next to Sarge.

"Sir. Yes sir," Tim said.

"Get under the table and suck one of those cocks down there."

Tim jumped under the table and looked at which cock he liked best. Taking the redhead's dick, he started to nurse on the head as he knelt under the table.

"Suit!" Sarge yelled.

Suit jumped up from licking some ash off the floor from Madame Woo's cigarette and knelt in front of Sarge.

"Get your scrawny ass under the table and suck cock."

The slave slipped quickly under the table and took Bobby's rigid cock in his mouth.

As Sarge pounded butt, he announced. "Let's see who can suck cock better. You two under the table, which ever of the two of you sucks out more loads from these rookies in an hour you'll get half my poker winnings."

Bull chimed in, "Who wants in on the pool? Ten bucks to get in."

Bull was busy drawing a chart as the men lined up at the bar with their cash in hand.

"Put in how many loads the winner takes."

Each of the men filled in what they thought the number would be and handed Bull their money.

Tim and Suit were now in earnest of their cock-sucking. They grabbed the balls of the rookies and rolled them in their hands as their mouths worked the dicks.

The rookies were in bliss. Sarge was moving back and forth, fucking each of them while he puffed on a cigar. Once in a while one of the men watching the action would hand Sarge a shot of whiskey to slug down between butts.

Sean was getting close. His legs began to quiver and suddenly groaned as he shot down Tim's throat. Soon after, Bobby did the same just when Sarge switched to his butt to screw.

Sean was recovering but not for long when he felt Sarge's thick cock slam up his ass.

"Oh, wait. Wait I ain't ready," he exclaimed.

Sarge slapped his ass hard. "Wait for what? You're goin' to get the fuck of your life. You should thank me for fucking your scrawny cop ass."

"Shit it hurts. Fuck!" Sean groaned and held tight to the table.

Tim knew what he had to do. His mouth worked the cop's cock, he sucked it down his throat, Tim's tongue flicked at the piss slit and he swallowed the dick to massage more jizz out of the balls. The cock began to harden and the rookie's pleas soon turned to groans of pleasure.

Sarge pulled out and went to the other hole. The little tight pucker wasn't so tight anymore and as jizz dripped from Suit's mouth, the cop was already getting hard again.

"Yeah, fuck me. Fuck me good Sarge."

"I'll fuck ya rookie, I'll fuck the livin' shit out of you before I'm done."

"Yeah Sarge, fuck me. Fuck me good."

Sarge began to drill the hot ass of the rookie. He reamed him with his fuck-stick when he sunk his dick deep into the hot hole.

"You'll get fucked rookie. I'll have you beggin' for me to stop before I'm done."

Suit worked the cock in his mouth. He could feel it harden up right off. Bobby's cock went hard and suddenly shot another load in the slave's mouth.

"Fuck. Jesus fucking Christ!" the rookie yelled out.

"Give Suit another mark, Bull."

Bull made a mark next to Bobby's name. "That's two to one," Bull announced.

One of the men, holding down the table said, "That dark haired rookie. Look how his tongue hangs out. What a fucking slut he is. He ain't holding on the table, he's got his hands spreading his ass cheeks."

Another man at the table answered, "That sailor of Sarge's, he's got his work cut out that's for sure. Look at that boy suck."

Tim was determined. He worked on the redhead's balls, coaxing another load from the baby-makers. His lips pursed around the cock's base, nursing it like a starving calf. Sean moaned, long and hard. His cock jumped in its hot, wet, sailor mouth.

"Oh. Sweet Jesus," the Irish rookie yelled out and came in loads down Tim's throat.

Sarge switched quickly back to Sean so as to feel the sphincter tightened his grip on his dick. He wasn't disappointed.

"Mother-fuck. This fuckin' rookie got a butt tighter than a duck's ass," he bellowed and shot a load of spunk deep in Sean's gut.

The rookie was shaking. His cock was still being nursed by the sailor. Not for more spunk but to get another load out of him and fast.

Bobby, with his dark hair falling in a curl on his forehead, begged Sarge.

"Please Sir. Fuck me sir. Stick your dick back in my ass. Please, I want your fucking hot cock up my ass. Please?"

"Wolfe!"

"Yeah Sarge?"

"Help me out here and shove something up that rookie's ass for me. This here cunt got a god-damn death grip on my barracuda."

The big mean cop walked over to the ass of the rookie. He looked down to see the young cop pulling his ass cheeks apart, his fingers dug into his hot little butt-hole, finger fucking himself.

"You want to get fuck Rookie!" Wolfe yelled.

"Please Sir. Fuck my ass sir. I gotta have a dick up my ass. Please."

Wolfe took his leathered gloved hand and smacked the ass of the rookie cop.

"What did ya say, rookie?"

"Please Sir! Fuck my ass Sir!"

"You want me to fuck your scrawny ass rookie? Want me to shove my fucking dick up that hole of yours?"

"Please. Sir, please fuck me. I'm begging you to fuck me. Fuck me all you want. I'm begging you. Fuck me!"

"You'll get fucked, rookie. You can count on that."

Wolfe slapped one cheek and then the other. The rookie groaned and held up his butt for Wolf's hand to smack his ass.

"You fucking slut. If I had known what a whore you turned out to be, I would have pimped you to the Eastside gang. You'd like that wouldn't ya? Being fucked by gangsters."

"Oh, please whore me. Please sir."

The rookie shot in Suit's mouth just thinking about being the gang's slut whore.

"Another one for Suit."

Bull noted on the pad. It was now three to two, the bartender announced and Suit was still ahead.

One of the marines watching said, "That fucker came without any dick in his ass. Just Wolfe slapping his butt with a leather gloved hand and Suit sucking to beat the band. Shit I think he's gonna win."

Sarge slapped Sean's ass while he fucked him. "You here that sailor? Did you here you're losing. What kind of navy man are you? You gonna let a low life scum bucket of a whore win? Are you sailor?"

Tim sucked as if his life depended on it. He took that cock down his throat and rooted at the base for more. He tugged on Sean's balls and grazed his finger where Sarge's thick cock went in and out of the hot Irish hole.

The cock began to harden again. The rookie groaned and moaned like a two-bit whore. Sarge slapped the ass and rode that butt like it was a bronco in a rodeo. "Suck sailor. Suck that fucking dick and get another load out of him," Sarge yelled.

Wolfe shoved his thick cock up Bobby's butt. The thick veined dick sunk like pipe in an oil well.

"Yeah, fuck me. Fuck my ass sir. Ahh, yeah cock in my ass. Thank you sir. Thank you."

"You better blow another wad rookie if you want anymore of this cock up your ass. You hear me rookie. Shoot your fuckin' dick wad,"

Wolfe slapped the ass again and the rookie shot on command.

Suit sucked and sucked, his belly began to bloat with all the jizz and piss he took in during the night.

"Another one for Suit." Someone yelled out from the bar.

"That's two up on the sailor," Bull announced.

Tim was blowing the cock like a Hoover on a mission. He stopped fondling the balls and began to slap them back and forth. Then he batted the nuts on the left and then the right. He made them swing side to side and back and forth. They hit Sarge's dick going in out of the rookie's ass. They smacked Tim's chin busy sucking on the redhead's cock.

"Ahh, fuck. Fuck I'm cumming," the rookie announced.

Tim sucked the goo down his throat and worked even harder to keep the dick from going soft and to get another load out.

"Tim's catching up now," Bull announced.

"That's right sailor. Suck that mother-fucker's cock. You can do it Sailor Boy. Suck that dick!" Sarge smacked the ass again and at the same time, Tim smacked the rookie's balls.

"Shit! Fuck!" The redheaded rookie yelled and shot again.

"They're tied now," Bull announced.

Tim hummed on the dick. He worked the cock with a frenzy of licks and sucks. Down to the base and back up. Down and up his mouth went in whirlwind pumping action.

"You gonna let that sailor beat you? Are you, you fucking shit-for-brains. If you lose, I'll have you tied to the wharf so every Tom, Dick and Harry can fuck your worthless ass," Wolfe yelled out and slammed fucked the rookie's ass.

Bobby groaned. His head moved to the side, with his eyes glazed over. Drool seeped from the side of his mouth. Suit underneath had the whole dick down his throat and was playing around the rookie's hole where Wolfe's fuck-stick was reaming him good. Suit knew the rookie's brains were centered on his asshole and was determined to get another load out of him quick.

The dark haired rookie put his thumb in his mouth and nursed it like a pacifier. He gurgled and cooed, in another world, with big cop dick up his ass and a hot mouth sucking loads down a warm wet mouth.

O'Reilly walked over next to Wolfe who had his cock sunk in rookie's ass.

"If I had known that rookie like to get fucked so much, I'd have pimp him out long ago. Father Flannigan would have paid a pope's ransom for him, and the good fathers at St. Mary would have as well to fuck that ass."

Wolfe took his dick out of the hole long enough to slap it a few times against the ass cheek of the rookie before he slammed it back in.

"Fucker loves it. How are we going to feed him enough dick out on patrol?"

"We'll whore the bitch out," O'Reilly answered. "Drop him off at a warehouse I know and have him fucked till its time to take him back. We better cage him in one of the holding cells back at the station. That fucker may never show up for duty with an ass like that."

Wolfe slapped the side of the rookie's ass. "Fucker like this, he'd be fuckin' all the prisoners. Yeah, I can see he'll need his own cell. I have a few special clients that would like a taste of that ass while he's in a cage."

O'Reilly said, "Look at that ass of his. It glows like an alter cherub. I like how it bounces when ya fuck him. Mind if I have a go at?"

"Let's double fuck him," Wolfe answered, "I punch in and out, and then you shove that fuck rod of yours in there. We'll bang him like pile driving men."

O'Reilly pulled out his hard cock and when Wolfe pulled out, the big Irish cop slammed his prick home to the pubes.

Back and forth the two fuck the rookie. His pale white skin had the sheen of alabaster, and not a feather on the creamy flesh. Bobby seemed to glow, revel in his ass being screwed fast and hard by two different big dicks. One was a bit longer and the other a whole lot thicker. The Irish are known for big thick meat and O'Reilly seemed to have cornered the market.

Wolfe's cock curved upward like a cavalryman's sword. He used it like one too. When Wolfe shoved his meat up an ass, it would bang on the prostrate both ways, milking the gland. The men fucked by Wolfe always spewed a lot of cock snot. It felt like they were constantly on the verge of an orgasm. And Wolfe had slaves that begged, paid and prayed for him to fuck them. It looked to the crowd like he now had a new disciple, someone with a natural boy-cunt, ready to fuck day and night.

Bobby had an angelic face, so innocent, with a bouncing lock of dark hair on his forehead. The rookie's slender hips and perky little butt that jiggled and humped for more and bigger cock, reached for dick to fuck him. All the two older cops had to do was get close to the pucker and it gulped the cock in on its own.

Bobby yelled back to the two cops fucking him. "Fuck me. Please. Oh yeah, that's it. Fuck the shit out of me. Yeah, mother-fucker. Fuck my ass."

"Hear that," O'Reilly said to Wolfe, "Sounds just like the alter boy at St. Mary when the good father is done with Mass."

Wolfe lit up as if a light bulb went on. "Ya know what!"

"No what?"

Wolfe slapped the ass he was fucking real hard, leaving a red welt on the cheek.

"This fucking rookie is double timing us. He's the alter boy I was telling you about, that I fucked silly."

"He does look innocent enough. Shit, I know he has to be at least twenty-one. How the hell did he get on the department if he wasn't?"

"I think it's him, the alter boy getting fucked at St. Mary. He just lives for it. Look at the face. He's in fuckin' heaven, with a dick up his ass."

"You know what, you're right. He is the alter boy at St. Mary. Well, he's gonna make us a nice little income. Put him in uniform and sell his ass, he'll get younger by the day the way he loves cock."

The dark haired rookie shot again. His load squirted around Suit's mouth that had a surprised look nursing the dick juice that shot with such force.

"Suit's up by two!" yelled out Bull.

"That fucker is gonna win if you don't get to sucking Sailor Boy." Sarge slapped the side of Sean's ass. "I'm doin' my part sailor. I got my gun dead center on the bull's eye, Sailor Boy. You better stop fucking off and get some loads out that rookie. I'm not going to tell ya again sailor. Suck that fuckin' dick."

Tim began to sweat. His mouth wrapped around the dick. He began to shove his lips deep down on the cock. He would swirl his head as he came up on the rookie's dick. His tongue lapped and slurped everywhere it could reach. Sarge's cock humped the rookie's hot hole. He would churn Sean's guts with his marine dick when deep in the hole. Tim's head moved so fast it was almost a blur, like some kind of suck machine on high, his mouth piston the cock like a jack hammer.

"Fuck!" cried out the redheaded rookie. "Fuck, I can't take it. You're fucking my brains out."

Tim's cheeks bulged out with all the seed the rookie pumped in him. Tim squirted it out the side of his lips, the cock juice dripped like honey on hot biscuits from the sailor's mouth. He let the joy juice fall on his hands and massaged the two orbs with their own hot fuck juice.

Sean's groans went on with Sarge never letting up on the rookie's ass. He pounded and ground his rod in the redhead's hot hole.

Tim never stopped his machine gun assault on the rookie's cock. His head pumped up and down on he cop's dick with rapid fire accuracy.

Sean's whole body tightened. "Oh fuck. Fuck me. Yeah fuck me!" he yelled back to Sarge who had a smile and the cigar clenched tight in his mouth.

Another load smacked against Tim's tonsils. It was as big as the first one and again Tim drained his cheeks of cock juice down the sides of his mouth and to his hands waiting to massage the goo into the cop's balls.

Shit, I ain't never seen someone load a gun so fast. That fucker must have emptied one nut and then the other," someone said next to Sarge.

Bull announced the tally. "It's even and there's only five minutes left on the clock, cock-suckers."

Tim and Suit worked hard on the dicks in their mouths. The men worked hard pumping their pricks deep in cop hole.

The dark haired rookie shivered and reached back to feel the slick cocks go in and out of his ass. He touched his ass-pussy lips, stretched around the thick, veined dick pumping his hole. Then he brought the tips of his fingers up to his mouth and licked them before going back for more.

"Hey, Suit!" yelled Wolfe, "Wake this slut up. Yank his fucking nuts until I hear him moan. And suck, you lazy cock-sucker. Suck!"

Suit grabbed the nuts of the cock in his mouth and pulled down hard. He didn't hear a moan that would satisfy Wolfe, so he pulled harder. The cock in his mouth started to grow stiff again.

"I don't hear him groanin' ass-hole."

Suit pulled harder with one hand and with the other began to smack the nuts. The sound of the balls being slapped and the banging of butts being fucked matched the cock-suckers slurps on hard cop dick.

The clock was down to three minutes. The two rookies looked like whores for a gang. Their tongues stuck out like panting dogs. Their holes were slick with jizz and dripped cock juice in long goopy strands to the floor.

Bobby was slapping his own ass. Suit was banging at his nuts while Wolfe and O'Reilly fucked him good and deep.

Tim's head was riveting the cop's dick in his mouth. He twisted the slimed up nuts and kneaded them with his knuckles. Sarge reamed Sean with his legendary marine cock. Once in a while, he would cum in the ass to keep it lubed. The floor beneath them had a puddle of cock-snot and ass juice, slick as vanilla pudding.

The two rookies groaned like jilted whores. Tim was still working the cop's dick like a woodpecker on steroids. Suit was a natural sucking machine. He could slide down the meanest cock and root for more at the base. He kept slugging the cop's nuts in his hand as he yanked and pulled on them with the other.

"Thirty seconds left," announced Bull.

The dark haired rookie was wild eyed. His ass was being plugged fast and hard. Each time his nuts were slugged, he would yell and his dick would jump in Suit's mouth.

Tim was working Sean's nuts. He sucked so hard that his cheeks caved in around the cock in his mouth. Sarge held the base of his dick and pushed it in a circle inside the ass of the rookie.

When Sarge felt the cop's prostrate, he jabbed it with the head of his cock.

"Fuck. I'm gonna shoot." The redheaded cop yelled out and shot another load that squirted around Tim's mouth.

"Times up," yelled Bull.

"Shit, I'm cumin'. I'm cumin'," screamed Bobby.

"To late, ass-hole," Bull yelled.

"Damn it. I hate loosing," Wolfe yelled and pulled out his dick.

"Suit get off that dick-head and clean my cock," O'Reilly barked.

Suit scrambled to get out from under the table. He scurried over to O'Reilly and took his cock in his mouth and started to lick it clean.

"Where's my Sailor Boy," Sarge asked.

Tim came out from under the table and went over to Sarge. The marine grabbed the sailor and gave him a bear hug, holding him off the ground.

"Is this the best god-damn cock-sucker in the entire fucking navy, or what!" yelled Sarge. "Bull! Drinks for everyone, and especially for Sailor Boy. Give him a double."

The crowd roared and ran to the bar for their free drink.

"Who won the pool?" someone asked Bull.

"Let's see. I'll be damn. It's Madame Woo."

Bull took the money and handed it to Madame Woo who quickly counted it and put it in a hidden pocket of her long sleeve.

"Thank you boys. Very nice. Bull give them another around of drinks on the house."

The men, who at first looked disappointed, now smiled and cheered the winner, lifting their drinks.

"To the winners!" one of the men said.

"To the winners! The crowd shouted back.

Tim burped up some jizz and caught it on the side of his arm before it ran down his mouth.

Wolfe and O'Reilly took the two rookies by the scruff of their necks.

"So you two are the dear little alter boys that Father Flannigan is always bragging about. And you never told us," O'Reilly said holding Sean and slapped his ass with the side of his billy club.

"Acting like little angels on Sunday and then you go on duty on Monday and you're a big tough rookie cop." Wolfe said, taking his belt from his pants.

The big German cop held Bobby's shoulder and smacked the folded leather belt across the rookie's ass.

"You didn't tell me you're a fuckin' whore. You didn't let me know I could have been making a mint on your baby-face that has probably sucked more dick than an eighty year old whore."

O'Reilly shoved his billy club up Sean's ass and left it there. He took his cuffs off and cuffed the rookie behind his back. "Get on your fuckin' knees and suck my dick."

The rookie carefully got to his knees with the billy club sticking out of his ass and waited for O'Reilly to give him dick.

"Start using your mouth, you fuckin' Irish whore."

Sean nibbled at the head of uncut cock. His tongue went into the piss slit and all around the foreskin. The rookie's tongue slipped under the foreskin and licked.

"You keep that stick up your ass rookie. I know it must be hard, as loose as it is after Sarge reamed you."

"Well Sailor Boy, you get half of my poker winnings."

"Gosh Sarge. I would do it for nothing if you asked me."

"I know you would. You're hundred percent navy and I'm proud of you."

"Gee Sarge, that's the nicest thing anybody has said to me."

Sarge put his arm around the sailor and toasted him. "What are you going to do with your winnings?"

Tim looked at the glass of whiskey for a while and then said, "Gee Sarge, I don't know. Can I take you out to a steak dinner?"

Sarge puffed on his cigar and smiled. "Sure you can sailor. We'll have ourselves a good time. Just me and you."

"That would be great Sarge. I would love it."

"We'll go to one of them fancy places that's got linen napkins and good booze."

"You tell me where Sarge and we'll go there."

"Well I better keep your winnings, seeing how you're not in uniform right now. How's that throat of yours?"

"Fine Sarge. That double shot you bought me made my throat all kind of numb."

"That's good Sailor Boy, cause we don't want to end the night just yet. Do we?"

"No sir, I'm having too much fun to go back to the ship."

"That-a-boy, sailor."

Sarge looked around as his hand drifted down the sailor's back to his butt. Sarge squeezed one of the sailor's ass cheeks and then gave it a light slap before his fingers went into the groove of Tim's ass and felt the sailor's pucker.

"Damn Sailor Boy, that little butt-hole of yours tightened up real fast. After fucking that rookie's sloppy hole I could use a nice tight fuck."

Tim looked at Sarge with stars in his deep blue eyes, "Gee Sarge, you say the nicest things to me."

"Ah, you know I'm sweet on ya."

"Me to, sir. I mean, I think the world of you too. Man to man like."

"We're military men through and through. Aren't we buddy?"

"We sure are sir. Through thick and thin, we're dedicated to the core."

"That's right sailor. Why you're the best damn cocksucker the navy has. Hell, you're the best cocksucker in uniform."

"Gee Sarge you're gonna make me blush."

"You go ahead and blush sailor. I like the way your cheeks get that rosy-red color."

O'Reilly had the two rookies on their knees next to each other. Their leather belts, from their pants, were around each of their necks, like a dog's collar and leash. In front of them were a line of men waiting for blowjobs. When either Wolfe or O'Reilly felt the rookie had enough cock to suck, they would yank the self-made leash with a jerk and pull the sucking rookie's head off the cock. Then the next man would step up and the guy who just had his dick suck would go to the back of the line to wait his turn for another blowjob. It didn't take long for the line to move. Each man got a short blowjob that kept their dick hard enough to stay up before it was their turn at the rookie's mouth.

If O'Reilly or Wolfe thought that either of the rookies weren't doing a good enough job, the rookie got smacked on the back of the head or a kick to the rookie's ass. The two young cops didn't seem to mind, they were more concerned about having a dick in their mouth, than the yank of the leash or the smack and a kick to their ass.

O'Reilly said to Sean, the redheaded rookie, "Now if you two alter boys get good at sucking dick, we might let you two get fucked in the ass. But you're gonna have to show us you're worthy of a good gang-bang."

Wolfe added, "Or we'll hog-tie you at the end of the wharf and you can help Suit take care of the derelicts. You wanna suck stinking wino cock? Then you better suck good, cause from what I hear, they have fleas as big as cockroaches."

O'Reilly piped in, "They are cockroaches, they eat the caked on scum off the wino's balls"

The two older cops laughed at their joke and then smacked the back of the rookie's heads before they pulled on their leashes for them to get off the cock and take the next one in line.

"Suck you son's of bitches. Suck that cock like it was your mother's tit." Wolfe yelled before he took his belt to the backs of the two rookies. He whacked one with the belt and then the other. The two rookies knew better than to take their mouths off the cock that was down their throat no matter how hard they were kicked

side of the face, it left a red welt on his cheek and the noise of the dick slap could be heard all over the bar.

"You fuckin' cop. You think you can shove someone like me around when you in the uniform. Now I'm gonna choke you on Jamaican dick man."

He shoved the cock down the rookie's throat and watched the young cop's face turned blue before he pulled his dick from the throat.

"You like that white boy? You like big Jamaican dick down your cock-sucking throat? Yeah, I can tell you do. I know what a faggot like you needs. You need dick all the time. Don't you? You white boy whore."

The dark haired rookie looked at the large Jamaican with the man's cock stuck deep down in his throat. The Jamaican watched the rookie cop. He watched to see beads of sweat form on the rookie's forehead. The dockworker shoved his hips forward a bit more. He smiled to see the young cop's lips stretched around his ebony prick, slick with phlegm coughed up from deep down in the rookie's gut. The Jamaican's sneer was an evil grin. He pushed the python cock even further down the throat. He watched the young cop's stomach swell when he started to piss. The rookie never felt the hot flow of urine, only that his belly began to swell out and that he desperately needed a breath of air.

Wolfe broke into an evil grin himself. He took the belt and played it on the rookie's back. The rookie sucked in more of the mammoth cock rather than air. There was still a good handful of big thick Jamaican dick yet to go.

The Jamaican reached out and grabbed the back of the cop's head and when Wolfe struck again, he shoved the rest of the horse cock down the rookie and watched fear grow across the young cop's face.

Then the most amazing thing happened. The Jamaican lifted the cop off his knees and up on his toes by making his cock twitch inside the rookie's guts. The large dockworker grabbed the base of his prick, taking both of his big hands where the cop's lips were fastened to his dick and forced the cop off the floor. There he hung with the giant fuck stick stuck deep down him and his legs dangling off the floor.

The dark haired rookie's legs kicked for a while, his hands beat at the air wildly and his pleading eyes looked into the face of the Jamaican for mercy.

The ebony dockworker smiled and watched the rookie weakened and his body go slack from lack of air. Then the young cop slid off the cock shoved deep in his gullet, slick with his gut juices. It took a while before his throat dislodged from the python of dick shoved deep in him. But when he did, his body collapsed on the floor, passed out.

The Jamaican laughed to see the cop unconscious at his feet, lying in the semen that was pumped into his mouth earlier. Suit began to lick his face to revive him and to get some of the fresh cum and piss the Jamaican left behind.

Sean, from the corner of his eye watched the whole thing and fear gripped him when the Jamaican looked his way. The redhead began to work in earnest on the cock in his mouth. The rookie prayed that the same fate didn't await him. He sucked in desperation, as if his life depended on it. He tried everything he could think of to satisfy the ten inch dick, which was tiny in comparison to the Jamaican's anaconda.

The ebony man turned his attention to Sean. He stepped right next to him, towering over the shaking rookie. Then the giant of a dockworker bent down and put his face close to the rookie's ear. He watched the young cop suck on a dick.

"Man, you don't think I didn't notice you? Hey man? You don't think I saw you look at me and my big prick?" The Jamaican lifted his cock that hung between his knees.

"You want to ride the pony white boy? You want to go for a ride on my donkey dick?"

The Jamaican swung the cock side to side like a pendulum. The rookie could hear the whoosh of air as it past. His eye strained to watch the pride of Jamaica swing by.

"You want that dick don't you white boy. You want to hang from it like your little friend, don't you cocksucker. I know you do, white boy. I know you want this cock more than anything."

He laughed a deep rich laugh and watched the young cop start to whimper.

O'Reilly smacked the back of the rookie's head. "Would you look at that? A fine Irish boy like you and after the blessed saint rid them from the emerald Isle. St. Patty would roll over in his grave, thinking an Irishman would be afraid of snakes."

The big Irish cop grabbed the back of the rookie's head and pulled the young cop's head off the dick in his mouth. He forced the rookie to face the big, black cock.

O'Reilly yelled at him. "Lick it, rookie. Lick that fuckin' python for a cock you fuckin' dick-wad."

The big cop forced Sean's tongue all over the slicked up dick. The puffy lips, from sucking cock, ran along the veins with his tongue slicking the way. The rookie could smell its heady aroma, the heat of black cock that called to him.

"I knew it. Once these white boys get a taste of chocolate, they never go back to vanilla," said the Jamaican.

Sean no longer needed O'Reilly to guide his mouth over the fleshy cock. He plied long licks, starting at the piss slit and up to the wiry pubes. He grabbed the Jamaican's dick and held it in both hands to savor every part, the veins, the head, and its massive size. The rookie's tongue glided along the fleshy cock. He rubbed his cheeks and lips on the phallus that he worshipped.

"He wants that dick now don't he?" said the Jamaican. "That right, white boy? You want this big ole cock in your mouth?"

The rookie gave him a pleading look before his lips went to the head of the cock and began to suck on it. Holding the cock in both hands, his mouth nursed on the head that filled his cheeks with big, black dick. The rosy red lips stretched around the girth. His pale freckled face, contorted to fit the python size prick in his mouth.

The Jamaican leaned his hips in for the rookie to take more cock. Once the young cop started to suck in earnest the black dockworker pulled it out and waved it in front of the rookie.

"Beg white boy. I want to hear you plead for this dick of mine."

Sean looked up with pleading eyes. Drool fell from his lips near the tip of the ebony cock inches from his mouth. "Please let me suck it." He said in a whimper.

"What you say boy?"

The rookie cleared his throat and said in a louder voice, "Please sir. Please let me suck your cock."

"Well, I don't know. You don't suck as good as your boyfriend. Maybe I should stick it up your ass instead."

Sean's sphincter tightened. "Oh, no Sir. I can suck your cock better than Bobby. I can suck it real good."

The Jamaican kicked the black haired rookie that lay on the floor. The young cop groaned and woke up. Dazed he looked around until his eyes cast on the Jamaican.

"Your boyfriend says he can suck this dick better than you. Is that true white boy?"

The dark haired rookie got up on his knees and grabbed the ebony cock. He began to suck on it immediately using both hands to hold it up to his face.

"Ahh," said the Jamaican. "Now that's a blowjob."

The redhead scooted over next to the other rookie. He tried to grab the dick from him but Bobby wouldn't let go. Then Sean leaned over and began to lick the chocolate colored balls as if they were Easter eggs. He pressed his face in and opened his mouth wide to get one of the balls. When it plopped inside, he sucked and licked, making it shiny when he released it and went for the other nut.

"That's it white boy, churn those baby factories for me, get them all hot to give you that juicy seed of mine."

The Jamaican patted the head of the dark haired cop. "You gotta have that dick. Don't you boy. Got to have my big fat prick in you all the time. You want to eat it. Huh boy? You want to eat my fucking cock?"

His hand caressed the side of the sucking mouth. The cop's nose began to goo with mucus. It bubbled down the sides of his chin and dripped in gobs with his gorging on the fuck stick in his mouth, throat, and gut.

Sean was smeared now in cock fuck juices and the other cop's spit. It smeared his face and red hair while he sat between the legs of the dockworker and sucked on his nuts.

"Suit! Where the fuck is that white boy? I need his nasty tongue up my big black butt."

Suit was kicked in the ass where he was holding a cigar in one hand and his mouth open for the ashes. The man whose cigar he held grabbed it before his ashtray left.

"Get your tongue up there white boy. Get me all worked up to nut and blow the back of this cop's head off with a load of good Jamaican nut juice."

Suit rammed his tongue up the Jamaican's butt. He took his hands and spread the sweaty ass cheeks and buried his mouth right to the pucker.

"Yeah. That's it, there's nothing like getting sucked—balls, cock and asshole, all at the same time. You fuckin white boys do a fine job. Work my fuckin dick bitch. Get your fuckin mouth down on it. Suck my balls white whore. I want to feel them down your cop throat."

The Jamaican reached behind him and ground Suit's face into his meaty ass. "You can play with my tonsils from where you are, you motha-fuckin piece of corporate shit."

Suit's face was turning crimson from lack of air. He spread the cheeks even further and shoved his tongue so far in that his lips pried the chocolate rosebud open.

"Yeah, eat my ass fucker. Eat it good," the Jamaican growled while he kept his hand pressed on the back of Suit's head.

The two rookies were sucking cock and balls. Sean forced the other cop from the dick and took over. The redhead nursed the head of the prick while his buddy ran his tongue up and down the length of the rod. As soon as the dark haired lad saw Sean near the tip of the head he forced the rookie off and took over, making the redhead go back to the balls.

The dockworker had his eyes closed, his legs spread wide. He began to grunt and moan when suddenly he shot his wad over the two cops fighting for his dick, trying their best to snatch the flying cum from the air with their mouths.

When the ebony man squirted the last of his load, all three servicing him, dived for the spunk that hit the floorboards, licking up the massive amount of spooge.

"Shit. Would you look at that, they're like hungry dogs fighting for a bone," one of the men watching said.

The Jamaican walked over to the bar and sat on a stool. "Bull. Hey man, give me a shot of rum. Those white boys just about suck me dry."

Sarge had Tim sitting on his lap. The sailor was nestled in the marines arms cooing as the sergeant flicked one rubbery nipple and the other. When he had both nubs perky and hard, he nibbled on them with his mouth. It made the sailor whimper and antsy. Sarge's big cock boned beneath the sailor's ass and quickly, Tim eased up to let the boner slip into his butt. He eased down on the prick until his ass cheeks once again rested on Sarge's lap.

"Feel better sailor? Like having that big marine cock up your ass don't you. I know you do and it fits real well don't it?"

Tim murmured that it did and pulled the marine's shirt open so he could suck on Sarge's tit. The drill sergeant let him, fiddling with the sailor's hard little nipples as well. He bounced the sailor on his lap a couple of times. Sarge had Tim unbutton his shirt the whole way and lifted his arm so that the sailor could bury his nose in the sergeant's pit.

The sailor took a big whiff and began to lick the salty black hairs of Sarge's armpit. It excited Tim and he started to bounce on the cock planted in his ass by himself. Now he straddled Sarge's lap facing him. His head buried in the heady aroma of sweat and musk as his tight little beach-ball buns bounced on Sarge's lap.

"Hmm. I love your dick up my butt, Sarge. You'll fuck me good, won't ya Sarge? You won't send me back to my ship without a belly of your baby batter. Will Ya?"

Sarge was working one of Tim's nipples, flicking it back and forth, watching it bounce back for another flick.

"Sarge will fuck you good. Have I ever disappointed you before, Sailor Boy? Huh. Has Sarge let my navy man down? Fuck no. I'm going to fuck you, hell, the whole damn place is going to fuck you more than once before you get back on deck, sailor. Yeah, Sarge will fuck you good all right."

Sarge turned to the guys around him at the table and said, "Ain't that right boys."

"Hell yeah," they answered.

Sarge's lips almost touched Tim's ear. The marine felt the heat coming off his hot little sailor as he whispered, soft and slow, "You like riding that big fat fucker? You like having big, fat marine cock shoved up your ass? Tell me sailor. You can't get enough military cock up that tight, white bubble ass of yours. Can you sailor."

Tim ground the cheeks of his ass at the base of Sarge's fuck stick. His head buried in Sarge's armpit with his tongue busy cleaning every inch of the musky pit. His small body rubbed against the sergeant, it glistened in sweat that coated them both.

"Please Sarge. Please keep fucking me. It feels so good. Feels like I got cock all the way up in me. I can almost taste it."

"You must have a gallon of fuck juice in you now, Sailor Boy." Sarge bounced the sailor's buns on his lap. He rabbit fucked the hole with short, fast, thrusts.

Tim burped. "Pardon Sarge. Oh, that's it, that's my love spot."

"Your whole ass is a love spot, Sailor Boy. You get hard eating a hot dog, you fucking navy whore."

Tim looked up at Sarge. "I do if it's your hot dog."

Sarge smiled and shoved Tim's face back into his pit. He nestled the sailor's butt cheeks on his lap and took a piss deep inside the navy man's ass. Tim's stomach bulged as his gut filled with hot marine piss.

"Sarge, I feel so full."

"I know you do little buddy, I got to clean you out to make room for more spunk. Now you sit there while I carry you to the head."

"Sure Sarge."

The big marine stood up with Tim's ass plugged with thick marine cock and walked him into the bathroom. He went to a toilet and sat down.

"Now, when I lift you up, you squirt in the can. Got it?

"Aye, aye sir."

The marine lifted the sailor up and as soon as Tim's asshole cleared the head of his cock he sat Tim back down with his butt-hole between the sergeant's spread legs. A whoosh of liquid came out of Tim's love tunnel. He squirted gobs of cock glue and piss until his belly went down and he relaxed in the arms of the sergeant.

"Don't that feel better?" Sarge asked.

"It sure does Sarge. I feel empty now."

"And we're going to do something about that too," Answered Sarge as he shoved his prick back up the sailor's ass.

"That's better Sarge," Tim said with a smile.

Sarge walked him out with his cock still shoved up Tim's ass. The marine walked over to the bar and had Tim bend over the bar. Then Sarge ordered a drink for both of them. While he fucked the sailor, slow and sure, Tim held on to the bar's top and tried to sip his whiskey between being rammed in the ass.

Sarge lit a cigar while he fucked. Once the cigar was lit, he held Tim's hips while he fucked him. "Yeah, that oil change did you good. I could ride this ass another ten thousand miles easy."

Bull was behind the bar and stood in front of the sailor. He dipped his fingers in the whiskey and then let Tim suck on his finger tips. Soon, the navy man had Bull's fingers all the way in his mouth and sucked on them like a cock. Bull would slip his fingers out, dip them in the glass of whiskey and then return them to the sailor's mouth for him to suck on like a nursing calf. The weighted pipe that stretched Tim's nuts hung down between his legs and swung back and forth like a pendulum with the steady fuck Sarge provided.

CHAPTER EIGHT

Bull was watching O'Reilly and Wolfe as they tied up the two rookies. The two rogue cops had the rookies knotted together, each sucking the other's prick. The rookie's legs and arms were folded and pressed around each other so that each rookie's ass was sticking out on either side in their tight, tied up sixty-nine position. There was the redhead with an ass above him on one end and the dark haired cop with an ass below his head on the other end. The two larger cops had tied them up hanging from the rafters, so that men could mount the butts on either end and the two rookies would swing back and forth on the dicks.

No sooner were they in place, and Suit had rimmed their asses to prime the holes for hot fucking, when a line on each end formed. All the men had to do was pull their cock out, shove it in an ass-hole and the back and forth motion would fuck the ass on their pole. The two rookies, with their mouths secured around the other's cocks, looked to see a dick enter the other rookie's ass from above or below. The redhead, Sean, had the view below.

"Okay men. Pick a partner. Let's see which pair has the better fucking motion. The team that can keep the stroke going the longest—wins. Oh, and you can't use your hands. You can't stop and if your dick comes out, you loose."

Wolfe and O'Reilly got on each end to show the men their newfound sport. Wolfe put his uncut dick at the entrance of the dark haired rookie's butt-hole. O'Reilly did the same with the redhead. On signal, Wolfe pushed his dick in and the two rookies swung tied together toward O'Reilly who impaled the redhead's hole with thick cop dick. When the creamy buns of the rookie's smashed against O'Reilly's groin, the Irish cop pushed his hips to send the two tied up rookies back on Wolfe's cock. In short time they had a rhythm going. The men could hear the sound of hot, bubble butt being slammed like a ping-pong match in China. Each rookie took a good ten inches of cop dick in the butt when slammed.

The redheaded Sean was mesmerized as he watched the German's big tough ass come into view. The cock would then pull off his buddy's ass-lips. The lips would cling to the side of the thick cop dick. Wolfe's balls dragged across his eyes and nose. He could smell the rank, stringent nut sack, the hairs tickling his face and lips where the other rookie's dick was implanted in his mouth. Sean's head, firmly tied in place, had no choice but to suck cock and watch as the German rutted the hole in front of his eyes.

The two beefy cops kept up quite a show. They volleyed off the last thrust and kept a fast tempo banging butts. But O'Reilly got hot with his dick pounding the hot tight ass and just before he came, he grabbed the ears of the dark haired rookie and crammed his dick in all the way.

"Fuck, that's good."

"O'Reilly! You, no good Irishman. You could have cost us the contest," Wolfe exclaimed from his end.

"Shit. Fuck that was some good riding ass I was pounding."

The two cops left and the next two men came up, both marines, one had a tattoo of a snake on his arm that coiled around and bit into a heart. The other had hair on his chest and arms that stuck out from his shirt. His face needed a shave, not that anyone minded in the bar.

"This here's gonna be a cinch to win," The tattooed man said, "We did this to a Saigon whore, she loved it."

The two men mounted the ass in front of them and began to pump butt. They worked up slowly, letting their cocks harden to their fullest before they began to volley back and forth, each taking a turn on pushing the ass on the other's rod. The marines had thick and mean looking cocks. The soldier with the tattoo had a prick that bent upward and pressed on the dark haired rookie's prostrate with each jab. Bobby, unable to move within the confines of the rope, began to grunt and spill cock juice into his buddy's mouth. It seeped around Sean's lips as he tried to gulp most of it down his throat.

The pounding went on though, but the tattooed marine was faltering. "God-damn this son-of-a-bitch," He exclaimed. "This fucker's hole is a whole lot hotter than that whore's. His fucking ass-cunt is grabbing my dick. It feels like he's sucking my dick with his ass."

"That's just him shooting from your bent rod, Sam. Get a grip and concentrate," said the marine fucking Sean's ass.

"Easy for you to say. Bet that Irish kid you're screwing has been fucked by half the Vatican, you should feel how tight this fucker is on this end."

"Well the other half was fucking your boy, so what's the problem?"

The dark haired rookie was ready with another load to feed the mouth tied fast to his cock. He whimpered and sweat began to bead on his forehead when suddenly another explosion of cock glue splattered Sean's tonsils. That sent the marine, Sam into a sexual frenzy.

"Fuck. Damn I can't take it, the fucker made me shoot my fuckin wad way too early. You fucker, I'm gonna make sure you pay for this ass-hole," he said when he grabbed the ass with his hands to hold it and pump the rest of his load deep in the butt.

"Damn you Sam and your bent dick. No more cop ass for you anymore, it just drives them crazy to have that rod of yours up their butt."

"You're just sore because you didn't get a nut."

"I'll get my nut alright. In your ass!"

The two marines walked off toward the head as two construction guys took their turn.

"Bull!" Someone asked from the crowd.

"What the fuck do you want?"

"Who has the best time?"

"The two cops, so far."

"I thought so, bet it's because they've been fucking these two for a long time."

"Naw," said someone. "It's because they use their dicks for clubs and got no feeling in them."

Laughter sounded out from the crowd.

"Hey, shut the fuck up. We don't want anyone breaking our concentration," said one of the construction workers who had just pushed his dick into one of the rookie's holes.

"Okay Billy-Bob, you just keep that hammer of yours in the hole and we'll win," said the guy's partner.

Billy-Bob's cock was unusually thick. It looked to be as thick or thicker than his dick was long, and it was a good length. He had to jab at the tight hole of Sean's ass a few times before the head went in.

"Jesus," said someone in the crowd. "Looks like the guy is laying sewer pipe in the redhead's ass."

One of the men closest to Billy-Bob said, "He smells like he's laying sewer pipe too." Then he moved a bit further away.

Sean's cheeks bulged out as he grunted a scream. The cock buried in his throat, dulled its sharp ring. The rookie's ass cheeks were spread, the hole stretched to a thin pink ring around the girth of the cock's head. With each slam from the other end, the cock's width stretched the hole more. And the hole began to fit around the cock tight as a latex glove.

It was like pounding nails until the dick hit flush with the hole. The stretched ass-lips clung to the cock when Billy-Bob pulled his monster part way out. It looked like the hole was being turned inside out.

Billy-Bob's friend on the other end said, "Dang it Billy-Bob, you ain't shovin' that ass hard enough."

"I'm doin' the best I can, the damn hole won't stretch out for me to send it off."

"You been corn-holin' the livestock back at the farm haven't yuh."

"Shit, if they stand still long enough, I get my pecker in pretty damn good."

The sphincter seemed to just stay in place near the base of the thick dick. The rookie's guts pulled out of his ass and then folded in with each stroke but the dick was just stuck at its base with ass ring clinging to it.

"I ain't feelin' anything, George," Billy-Bob said as he tried to keep his hard.

"Spit on it sum, Billy-Bob."

The red-neck hocked up a loogie and spat at the hole where it clung to his cock. Then Billy-Bob wrapped fingers from both hands around the base of his dick and pushed the guts back in.

"Disqualified," yelled out Bull.

"Dang you Billy-Bob and that tree trunk of a dick of yours."

"Ain't my fault it's wider than it's longer."

Billy-Bob pulled his cock out and with his fingers, pushed back in the rookie's ass-lips and gave them a pat.

"Fucker was sure good and tight though. I bet if I had time, I could make that butt jump on my dick."

"Shit. Stick to the mares, Billy-Bob, or you'll stretch all to hell any good man-pussy you put that club of yours in," said George.

As the two walked away to see how well they did, one of the men standing nearby looked closely at the stretched hole.

"Shit. I think this hole is out of commission, the only thing that will fill it is a fire plug."

The man next to him said, "I think I heard an echo, Ralph."

Wolfe walked over to the rookie's hole. He took his belt and smacked the ass lips until they swelled up. "That should tighten this pussy's hole."

Two other men took their places at each end of the rookies. Tears were streaming down Sean's face after the belt smacked his ass lips. The dark haired youth watched as the next dick went into the redhead's hole. It was long, but not wide. Hard with a slight bent upward.

Then he felt a cock enter his own hole. Short jabs at first until the man had his cock embedded inside him. He felt his ass-cheeks being smacked each time by the pubes surrounding the cock that sank in his hole. Sean, on the other end, never felt his butt cheeks hit flesh. It was as if a pole was up his ass. His hole glided along the length of the cock and then came back before another thrust sent the cock to skewer his ass again. No matter how hard the thrust, the dick never went in full length. Sean thought the cock in his ass had to be over a foot and half long. The dick never pushed back. His hole would glide off and then he felt the push from the other end just before his butt-hole filled with cock. No tickling pubes touched his butt-cheeks. No solid muscle slammed into the cheeks of his ass. Just the feel of his man-cunt gliding on the cock inside was the only thing he could feel of the man fucking him.

Sean hardened in the other rookie's mouth. The fucking he was getting sent waves of pleasure throughout his body and soon he shot his load in the mouth attached and held in place by the rope. He could hear his friend gurgle as he pumped his semen in the mouth. When he thought his orgasm was finished, the ride on the long cock got him hard again so that his dick never went soft. He just kept squirting in the mouth sucking his dick. With his ass gliding on the cock, not coming off the cock or feeling its root grind into his butt cheeks he felt as if he was a swing set and his butt the swing. He squirted freely into the sucking mouth on his prick and groaned with aching balls trying to squirt more dick wads out.

One of the men watching, commented, "Jesus, those two sure have a good rhythm going. Don't they?"

"Look at that guys cock. That dick of his looks as long as a yardstick."

The man with the long cock was thin and tall. His fingers were long and his nose was too. He watched his cock skewer the hot hole his dick was buried in. Watched it glide up the length but never making it all the way to his pubes before it reversed course and headed towards the head of his dick. It never made it to that end either. The head was still a couple of inches inside the ass before the guy on the other end slammed the butt he was fucking back on his long cock.

"God-damn that's good ass," The tall man said. "Good fucking hot cop ass. Nice and loose too. I could fuck like this all day. Fuck that cop's butt until the sun rose, if I wanted."

"Yeah," he said, "Fuck my cock, slut. You like that don't ya. You like having my big long dick up your butt, your ass-lips gliding on my fuck pole. Don't ya cop? Yeah, I know you do. I can see you want me to fuck you into tomorrow. What a fucking slut you are."

The tall man put his hands behind his hips and clasp them, shoving his hips out a bit and watched the butt glide the length of his cock. The dark haired rookie watched Sean being fucked as he sucked the rookie's prick. He watched the ass, close to his face, glide back and forth on the dick. It looked like the cop's ass-cunt was skewered on longshoreman cock. A fuck machine made to screw itself on cock. He sucked Sean's prick while the other man's fat dick pounded his butt. He wished he could feel what it was like to have the long cock up his ass, even though he enjoyed the cock in his. He sucked and swallowed the semen Sean shot in his mouth almost constantly and knew the redhead must be in slut heaven with the lengthy dick he had in him.

"Hank," said the tall man.

"Yeah Tom."

"Can you pump that ass a little harder? I want to see if it will go in to the pubes up this fine ass that's fucking my dick."

"Shit, I don't know. I'm slamming this ass pretty fucking hard. I'll give it a try."

Hank slammed into the ass, leaning a bit at the end to shove the butt forward more. On the other end, Sean's ass moved an inch or two closer to Tom's pubes but still didn't quite make it.

"Damn that's good. Good fucking ass," Tom exclaimed.

"I'm glad you like it buddy. I'm doing all the work on this end."

"Yeah, but it sure does feel good on this side, just to stand here and have this nice fine cop ass fucking itself on my cock."

"I bet it does buddy. Wished I had a cock that long. I could make some money on it selling the damn thing by the inch."

"Shit," someone in the crowd said, "You could sell that fucker by the foot. That's a fine looking piece of wood he's sportin'."

"Never had any complaints," Tom answered with a smile.

Sean was in a state of bliss. His body relaxed and his ass seemed the center of the universe to him. He could feel every inch of hot cock meat go in and out of his butt. He could feel the veins as they surged back and forth inside his hot hole. He wanted the cock to stay. He wanted the man fucking him to never stop. He sucked on the dark haired rookie's dick like it was the cock in his ass. He felt that they might meet somewhere deep inside him. He wanted to tell Tom how much he loved being fucked by him. That he would be his sex slave if he would have him. He would whore for him if he would only fuck him every chance the longshoreman got to stick that pole of his into his ass. It frustrated him that he couldn't remove his mouth from the cock in it, that he could express his joy of the dick in his ass. So he sucked the other's rookie's prick. Sucked it like he thought the tall man would want him to suck his dick, only the dick in his mouth wasn't near as long as Tom's. Sean wanted to pull his ass cheeks apart to get more of the cock inside. He wanted to sit on the long pole and ride that donkey dick for all it was worth. But he couldn't. Tied up, unable to move his arms or legs that were folded up along with that of the other rookie, he had to be content with the cock in his ass for as long as Tom could ride his hole.

Hank began to tire. His strokes were half hearted. He was near coming and wanted a break from shoving his hips back and forth.

"Tom, you fucker, you're going to have to work some. I'm getting tired doing all the work here. Why don't you take over a while so I can relax and have this hot ass on my prick fuck me for a while?"

"Well that ain't the way we planned it. Don't you want to win?"

"Sure I do, but I've been pumping for a good hour now, or more."

"If I slam that ass, bird brain, it might shove that butt off your dick. I've got a hose compared to that pecker of yours."

"Shit. I'll keep at it then. How much longer you think it will be before we win?"

"Don't really know. But we want the best time we can make don't we?"

"I guess you're right, but dang it's getting to be work on this end."

"Hank?"

"Yeah Tom?"

"Shut up and fuck."

It was music to Sean's ears. He could have his ass glide on Tom's dick the whole night long. The cock was the perfect size for him. Just thick enough and definitely long enough to satisfy him in every way.

Hank's ass began to spasm. "Ouch, damn it. Shit," he exclaimed while rubbing his muscled butt.

His beat began to waver. Hank's sweat poured from his body and fell around him to puddle on the floor. To distract his himself he started to smack his own ass cheeks. They turned a flaming red and the more muscle pain Hank had, the harder he smacked.

Bobby's face had a look of concern. He thought he might be doing something wrong, so he tightened his ass-hole on the cock fucking him. It seemed to work, the dick seemed to get bigger inside his ass. So he loosened when the cock was shoved deeper and tightened his ass on the out stroke.

Now Hank began to sweat for a different reason. Suddenly he was fighting not to shoot his load in the ass. Before it was just another hole but now it was prime ass. A good fuck.

"Shit Tom, I'm gonna shoot my load."

"Think of something else."

"This ass is good pussy Hank, better than pussy. I think this fucking butt is sucking my cock."

"Ass can't suck dip-shit."

"Well this one is."

"Think of your mother."

"It ain't working, I fucked my ole' lady."

"Damn you, Hank."

Hank was now fucking for the sheer pleasure of having his cock in a good hot fuck hole. He wanted to marry the rookie. It was the best fuck he ever had.

"God-damn it all to hell, Shit mother fucking shit," Hank yelled out.

The dockworker's body shook. He trembled out of control, shot his wad deep in the hot tight hole and collapsed over the two tied up rookies.

"Damn it all, Hank," Tom said.

"I couldn't help it. That ass of his was sucking my dick."

Bull announced from the bar. "Best time yet. One hour and twenty-two minutes."

"We might win after all," Hank said with a reassuring smile.

Sean was disappointed that the fuck was over. He soon felt another cock go in his ass and settled back down to suck on the other rookie's cock.

Sarge had Tim sucking his dick now while he sat on a bar stool and watched the contest. Suit was cleaning Sarge's boots with his tongue. Someone used a marker on his rear and made a target by drawing rings on his ass that made his butt-hole the bull's eye. Every once in a while, someone would throw something at the targeted ass of Suit, who just kept licking at Sarge's shoes.

All around Suit were ashtrays, shoes, beer mugs, cans, shot glasses and cigar butts. His ass was smeared with the remains of everything that hit him and the occasional wad of spit that came his way.

"Bull," said Sarge

"Yeah buddy?"

"Think I might get my dick in this little contest," he said as he glanced over to where the two rookies were being fucked by the next team.

"Well, you'd probably come out on top, being so good at that sort of thing."

"Yeah but who am I going to get for a partner? Now Sailor Boy here, he would shoot his wad in a second. Not that he wouldn't give it his best. He just ain't real good at holding his wad back."

"That is a dilemma Sarge. I can't think of anyone that would be good enough to keep up with you."

The two men were silent while Tim sucked and Suit licked. After some time passed, Sarge said. "What about you. We'd make a great team."

"That might work. I'll have to ask Madame Woo though."

"You go, Bull. Have Suit clean himself up enough to wait on customer first," Madame Woo interjected.

"Suit! Get your fucking lazy ass in the can and clean that shit off. You're gonna earn your keep for a change."

Suit scurried off to the head to clean off, while Bull poured a few drinks for the men that ordered them. Then the big man left his post and stood with Sarge as Tim still sucked on his cock.

The two men next to each other looked magnificent. Both by far the strongest and largest men in the place, they stood out as men among men. Admired by everyone and envied. The muscles in their arms popped out like cannon balls. Their chests stretched the shirts that contained them. Thighs of titans and beach ball buns, but what everyone gawked at and talked about were their legendary cocks. They both had big, thick, meaty cocks and bull balls. Their pricks when limp, which wasn't often, hung half way to their knees.

"What's the game plan?" asked Bull.

Rubbing his chin that was in need of a razor, Sarge studied the action where the two rookies were tied.

"What do you think about this idea," He said with a deadpan face. "We fuck the living shit out of the both of them. Then win."

"I like that idea," Bull answered.

"Well, I don't see these two clowns lasting much longer." Sarge said and pointed to the action going on in the middle of the room.

The two guys fucking the rookies were having a hard time of it. They had their dicks in the asses of the rookies but instead of fucking they were pissing while drinking beer. Their piss that didn't sink in the holes, instead dribbled around where their pricks were stuffed inside the butts. A puddle formed on the wood floor beneath the suspended rookies that mixed in with the ass juices of the well fucked rookies. The two men fucking them could hardly stand up anymore from being drunk.

"Shit, would you look at that, I ain't going to stand in all that crap to fuck. Suit!" yelled out Bull.

From the bathroom, the bar slave came running out. His naked body glistened from the water he had splashed on himself to clean up and knelt in front of Bull.

"Madame Woo?" Bull said.

Madame Woo had just finished placing an incense stick in the cauldron.

"Now what Bull?" She asked.

"I need Suit to clean up a mess. Can Sailor Boy here tend bar?"

Madame Woo looked at Tim servicing Sarge's cock, and then she turned back to Bull.

"If he can work the bar as good as he sucks dick. I don't see why not."

"Suit. Get your fucking ass over there and clean up that shit on the floor."

The slave crawled over to the mess under the two rookies and proceeded to lick at the edge of the puddle while the two men on each side of the rookies fucked.

It wasn't long before one of the men fell over with his dick still in the ass. His cock pulled out with a plop when the big guy fell and the ass-hole that it was in squirted piss over the back of Suit. His teammate on the other end wasn't aware they were disqualified and kept pumping with a drunken grin.

Bull yelled out, "It's over ass-hole. You lost. Get yer fucking dick out of that hole and let us pros in there. We're gonna show you all how to fuck cop ass."

Someone grabbed the guy's arm that was fucking the rookie and led him to the side with his cock swinging from the freshly fucked hole.

The two rookies were rocking like a pendulum. Ass juices dripped from their holes, and their mouths still had each other's dicks in them.

Sarge walked up to Sean's butt. He held his cock in his hand and used it to play with the hole in front of him. He tickled the ass-lips until his cock hardened and then shoved it in the cum slicked hole.

Bull went to the other side, he unbuttoned his fly, pulled out a cock that needed two hands to get it all out and shoved it full length into the rookie's butt. He heard Bobby, though he had a dick in his mouth, take in breath when he slammed his salami home.

The two men started to fuck hard right away. No easy in for them. They slammed the butts in front of them making the timber that the two rookies were tied to creak like an old sailing ship. Groins smacked ass and the butts reverberated from the hard muscled men that slammed into them. The young cops ass cheeks jiggled like jelly in a bowl and the pace was furious. The two powerful men acted as if the contest was between them on who could fuck the hardest. The rookie's eyes had a look of bewilderment in them. Their hair was tousled from being slammed back and forth and they seemed more intent on keeping the cocks in their mouths for something to hold on too rather than to suck.

"Fine ass for fucking," said Bull.

"This one is good, but it ain't trained like Sailor Boy's. This here ass ain't jumping on my dick."

"Shit Sarge, you're fucking it like you were at batting practice."

"Well it's what you got to do with an ass like this. How ya gonna feel anything otherwise?"

Tim was serving drinks and every chance he had, would look at Sarge with the eyes of a puppy dog. Suit was underneath the two tied up rookies busy licking the floor clean.

"Get over here Suit and lick my nuts for a while," Bull said.

The large orbs swung back and forth between Bull's legs. Suit reached up and grabbed them from behind. He held them in his hands and took long licks with his tongue over the hairy sacks. Bull's ass would come back and cover Suit's face and nose. He would inhale when the bartender's butt was in his face, savoring its smell. His dick hard, it dripped, adding to the sex juice he had yet to lick from the floor.

The two well fucked butts began to turn a crimson red from the constant slams into them. The ropes that held the rookies in place were strained from the workload placed on them. The knots tightened into tight fists of rope. Both rookies had a worried face evident though their mouths held cock. It seemed that the beams of the old bar on the wharf were being tested to see if they were sea worthy, in shape for a perfect storm.

The two men fucking didn't have the slightest concern about the creaking beams, or the ropes that held the hapless rookies in place. They didn't bother to notice the worried expressions on the two cops. Their only concern was the slamming fuck they delivered. Their ability to work as a team in fucking the two tied up cops.

"Sailor Boy!" Sarge yelled out.

"Yes sir," he responded.

"Get me a whiskey will ya."

"Sure thing Sarge."

Tim finished drawing the beer in his hand and poured out Sarge's favorite whiskey into a clean glass. He then brought it to Sarge in a hurry, not spilling a drop.

Holding it out to Sarge, he smiled when the marine looked at him and tousled his blond hair.

"Thanks sailor."

Tim beamed and said, "Sure Sarge."

The sailor watched as the sergeant fucked. He stared at the cock slamming into the redhead's ass.

"You're doing a fine job on the ass sir. A fine job if I don't say so myself."

"Jealous, sailor?"

"Well maybe a little. I can't help but wished it was me you were fucking."

"It can be sailor. Want me to tie you up like this and fuck you silly? Is that what you want sailor? Want Sarge to fuck you into Sunday? I will if you want. I'll fuck you for days if you'd like."

Sarge's hand played with Tim's ass, he shoved a finger up the sailor's butt and then put in another one. When he had finger fucked the sailor for a while to cause the navy man to bone, he pulled his fingers out and allowed Tim to nurse on them like a cock.

"Who do you have to fuck around here to get a drink?" Someone from the bar announced.

"Better get back to work sailor."

"Yes, sir."

Tim ran back to the bar and over to the man who wanted a drink. Once he was there and took the order, pouring him a fresh beer from the tap, he brought it to the man and placed it in front of him.

"Don't you think you owe me an apology for taking so long?" The construction guy said.

"I'm sorry sir to take so long to serve you." Tim answered.

"Well that ain't good enough. How about you sucking my dick?"

"I have to work the bar sir," Tim answered.

"Well, I think you owe me a good sucking for insulting me. Why don't you put those pretty lips around my salami and give it a kiss."

"I'll have to ask Sarge, sir. He may not like that."

The construction man grabbed Tim and pulled him over the top of the bar. Then he forced him down to his knees, pulled out his cock and shoved it in the sailor's mouth.

"Suck that dick, you fuckin' swabby."

"But…"

"I said suck my cock sailor."

The cock pushed against Tim's lips and he opened his mouth and let the construction worker's cock go in. The man had his fingers wrapped in Tim's curly blond locks, using the sailor's hair to guide Tim's head on his dick.

"I know a cocksucker when I see one and when I saw you, I said, now there's a fuckin' dick licker if I ever saw one."

The man's prick was large with a big head. The flesh that covered the cock was as tough as cow hide. The veins stuck out and wrapped around the girth of the dick. He made it plain that he was in control of Tim's mouth. Sometimes when his cock was buried to the hilt in the sailor's throat he would hold fast to Tim's hair in his hand and kept the sailor's mouth from coming up. Then he would relax his grip and let the sailor get some air before he shoved his mouth back down on the cock.

When he was ready to shoot, he grabbed Tim's hair with both hands and skull fucked the sailor.

"That's it cocksucker. Get ready to take my load, fag. Eat me faggot. Yeah, eat my fucking dick juice."

The man was rough with Tim. He was moving the sailor's head back and forth on his cock and with the other hand, he slapped the sailor's face, spitting on Tim while he backhanded the sucking sailor.

"Like that fag. You like being treated like scum don't ya. You dick licking perv."

Tim couldn't answer with the abuse to his mouth going on. The man didn't care. He used Tim's mouth as a hole for his dick to get off in. The guy was on the mean side of looks. With his construction hat on, its bright yellow contrasted well to the thick black hair that curled out from it. His face needed a shave, the cleft in his chin, his dark brooding eyes, made his handsome face take on that of a brute.

Tim looked up at the dark eyes of the hardhat. With the man's cock stuffed down his throat, his succulent lips, moist where the cock and mouth joined, nursed and sucked on the man size prick. Tim's big blue eyes pleaded, but the sailor's cock was stone hard. His throat held the mushroom head of the hardhat. He gulped on it, as if his throat sucked the head of the cock. His lips worked at the base of the shaft, imploring the cock for more meat.

"Yeah, cocksucker. Suck my fuckin' dick."

His head went back and he looked up at the wood beams with the smoked filled ceiling. The hardhat's legs tightened when he bent and shot his load down Sailor Boy's throat.

Tim's mouth gushed with the rush of jizz. His cheeks bulged first before his lips seeped the sticky cream. He gulped and forced even more cock juice down his throat. The jizz seeped from his nose, ran down the sides of his lips and still he kept gulping like a nursing calf.

Tim looked over to where Sarge and Bull were fucking. The two rookies being batted back and forth between the two studs, he looked to see if Sarge might see his cock was hard. Tim's nipples perked while cock goo dripped from his face down his chest and between his pecs where he rubbed it on his perky nipples. It was hard not to want the cock in his mouth or the jizm that seeped from it. He hoped that Sarge wasn't mad at him, for not fighting the bigger hardhat off. He decided to be patient and wait to see what happened, so he swallowed the semen of the hardhat and sucked on the man's dick for all it was worth.

When the hardhat was through with his ejaculation, he pulled out his cock and wiped it off in the blond curls of Tim's head. Then he slapped the sailor so hard that Tim fell over on his side. After that the hardhat hawked up a wad of spit and spat on the sailor's face.

Sarge kept his rhythm. He didn't seem to notice Sailor Boy on the floor with a wad of spit on his face, or the red mark on his cheek where he was slapped. Bull and Sarge kept up their assault on the two rookies. They fucked them as if it was an Olympic sport. Neither of them looked tired or about to slow down. Their dicks pumped in and out of the two cops fast and hard.

Tim lay on the floor. He felt his cheek where he was slapped. It wasn't the kind of slap Sarge would give him. It was a slap from someone mean and hurtful.

"Get back on your knees faggot. You're not finished yet," The hardhat barked.

Tim slowly pulled himself up to kneel once again in front of the hardhat. He looked up at the rugged face of the construction worker with tears in his eyes.

The hardhat raised his hand to strike Tim again. "Open your whore mouth, fag."

Tim opened his mouth and closed his eyes. He felt the man shove his cock back in before piss flowed down his throat. He swallowed as fast as he could, some of it dripped from his lips and down his chin.

"You're a fuckin' toilet. A pig," The construction worker said.

He kept pissing in Tim's mouth until he was finished. Then he pulled his cock out and used it to beat the sailor's face. When he was finished cock-slapping Tim, he back handed the sailor so hard that it left Tim sprawled on the floor next the construction worker's feet. Then the man raised his foot and smashed the sole of his work boot into Tim's groin.

"Faggots like you are scum. Fucking sea scum floating in a ditch."

He pressed harder on Tim's groin and worked the heel until Tim moaned in pain.

The sailor begged, "Please, stop."

The bully pressed even harder until he heard Tim groan in agony and tried with his hands to lift the boot off his genitals.

The hardhat removed his foot and grabbed Tim by his hair. He pulled him up and slapped him until he went limp. Then he turned the sailor around and shoved his cock deep in the sailor's ass, shoving him over the side of a chair nearby.

"When I'm finished with you, you'll know you've been fucked. Not like that pussy marine that's been sticking it to you."

The hardhat fuck was mean and brutal. The seaman shook from the attack. His hole, never given a chance to relax, felt a spasm of pain that he never experienced with Sarge. Tears rolled down the sailor's cheeks. His butt clenched trying to prevent the assault on his ass-hole. It did no good. The hardhat grabbed the sailor by his hair and forced his head back so that the man could spit on Tim's face again.

He called him filthy names, "You fucking, whoring, slut. Your mother was a whore and so are you. A piece of trash, a cunt, that's what you are. I'd have you thrown out of the navy. You're a disgrace to the uniform. You worthless piece of shit."

The construction guy was getting louder and the crowd looked nervous, knowing that Sarge must be hearing what the hardhat was saying and doing to Sailor Boy.

The only sound in the room was Sarge and Bull fucking rookie ass, and the hardhat's wicked butt-fucking and bad mouth.

Bull looked at the clock near where Madame Woo sat. They had another fifteen minutes to go to beat the record. He looked over at Woo's expression that was none too pleased, with no bartender on duty there was no money being made. Bull gritted his teeth when he looked over at where Sailor Boy was being butt-fucked by the hardhat and clenched his fists. He glanced at Sarge, who seemed not to notice what was going on or that the crowed had grown quiet. Sarge's eyes were riveted at the hole he fucked and, like the drill sergeant he was, fucked on until mission completed.

"Yeah ya fuckin' slut. I'm going to fuck you a new ass-hole boy," The hardhat yelled out. Then he slapped Tim hard on the cheek of his ass.

"I'll make that fuckin' cunt of yours so loose your hole will look like a tunnel."

Tim's tight buns were slapped red, their bubble cheeks, puffy and swollen from the abuse by the hardhat, jiggled with each smack. He held tight to the side of the chair with the muscles in his arms bulging with strength in their grip to stay fast. The sinewy muscles in his legs popped out like steel cables and his bubbled butt took the onslaught like a proud navy man in battle.

Bull looked back at the clock. Three minutes to go and they would win. He looked at Sarge.

"You thinking what I'm thinking?" He said.

"Damn right I'm thinking the same thing and when we're through here, we got some ass to kick."

"Oh yeah, Big time."

The two rookies were fucked silly. They just sucked like nursing babes on each other cocks and let their little butt-holes turn into cum-dumps for the men. Their faces were a mess of jizz. It ran out of their noses, dripped from their mouths, they were mindless fuck holes ready for any cock.

The crowd fixated on the clock. Once in a while, one would look to see if the hardhat had any idea the peril he was in. Oblivious, he kept up his verbal assault and his mean butt fucking with slaps to the sailor's ass that turned it from pink to red.

The crowd in unison gave the countdown. "Ten—Nine—Eight—Seven—Six—Five—Four—Three—Two—One!" They roared.

The bar went wild. Some men near Bull and Sarge grabbed the winners' hands and lifted them in victory.

"To the victors!" The men said.

CHAPTER NINE

Bull and Sarge walked over where the hardhat was fucking Tim. Sarge grabbed the hardhat by the neck. "To the looser!" he bellowed and pulled the construction guy off of Tim in a wink.

The hardhat dangled in the air, Sarge held him up by the back of his neck like a bad dog and shook him enough that the yellow hat bounced on the construction worker's head.

"Boy," said Sarge long and slow, "I'm going teach you some manners about keeping your filthy hands off other people's property."

The hardhat looked shocked. His cock dripped ass juice from the freshly fucked hole of Tim's. In his bewildered state, he looked out at the crowd as if someone might help him. All he saw were the eyes of men filled with lust.

"Look Sarge," he said in a pleading voice, "I was just having a little fun with Sailor Boy that's all."

"We can see that," said Bull. "You were fucking my bartender, Madame Woo is out some money, guess you want to buy a couple of rounds for the boys to make it up. Don't ya?"

"Yeah, sure Bull. Rounds for everybody!" The hardhat yelled out with a nervous laugh.

Tim stood up and looked at the two men who rescued him. His blue eyes twinkled and his dimpled smile came back on his smudged face.

"Get yourself cleaned up sailor. I got some business to attend to and you got some drinks to pour for the boys," barked out Sarge.

The naked sailor saluted, "Aye. Aye. Sarge," he said and ran off to the head to wash his face.

Sarge sat the hapless construction worker down and put his heavy arm across the man's shoulders. The hardhat was bent at the knees, sweat poured from his forehead.

"Now Sarge, I sure appreciate you letting me have a little of that fine tail of Sailor Boy. Mighty fine ass that boy has. And sucks like there's no tomorrow. Mighty fine of you."

"I didn't let you have a fucking thing, prick. You took what was mine and I'm not happy."

Sarge used the arm on the hardhats shoulder to squeeze his neck like a vice. The hardhat began to whimper.

Sarge's face got right next to the hardhat's ear and said, "What you gonna do for me, maggot?"

"Anything Sarge. You name it buddy, it's yours."

"I don't know if you have anything I want. Why don't you get up on this table here and take your clothes off. One piece at a time."

"Sure Sarge. Sure."

"Suit!" Bull yelled out.

Suit, still licking the floor, stood up and ran to stand in front of Bull.

"Put some strip music on, ass-wipe. We're gonna have a little show here."

Suit ran to the jukebox, selected some songs and ran back. The music played slow and easy, a sensuous bump and grind came out of the speakers.

"Okay pretty boy. Let's see you strip to the music." Sarge said.

The bewildered hardhat looked around and said to the marine, "Pardon Sarge?"

"Strip ass-hole and it better be entertaining. We got some nice music for you to shake that ass of yours too."

"Sure Sarge. Sure."

The hardhat looked at the crowd, he wasn't sure at first what to do when someone yelled, "Show us your tits, baby."

The stripper lifted his wife-beater on one side to expose a nipple to the beat of the music. The crowd hooped and howled, "More. More."

The construction guy began to get into it. He never had so much attention before and began to move his hips to the beat, lifting up part of his wife-beater on one side and then the other. He pulled up his shirt to expose both his pecs to the crowd that went wild. He slowly, teasingly, lifted the shirt over his hardhat and swung it around in the air to the music's sweltering beat. Then he flung the shirt to the crowd where they fought over the ripe, soiled tidbit.

The hardhat slowly unbuckled his pants. His butt shaking in their tight jeans, he shoved it out to the crowd and shook it.

"More. More," yelled the crowd.

The stripper pulled at his jeans on one hip and gave the crowd a shot of butt cheek. Then he pulled his pants back up and faced the crowd, pushing his groin out for their amusement as he slowly slid the leather belt from the jeans.

When it was free, he waved it to the crowd and threw it to them. Then he unbuttoned the top of his jeans. He took off his hardhat and placed it in front of his fly, moving it off and then back on to the beat. His dark curly hair glistened on the square jawed man. His face, unshaven, his high cheekbones made him look as rugged as any hardhat could look. The muscles in his arms popped out and shined with the sweat of his body.

He put the hardhat back on and with his pants now loose, turned around, pulled his jeans over the cheeks of his ass and had his ass-hole wink at the crowd.

They roared with delight and screamed for more. The hardhat was happy to provide them and pulled his jeans back up. Turned around and open the fly of his pants. His jock sprung out, filled with a hard dick and big nuts. The crowd roared again.

Tim had cleaned himself up and was serving drinks as fast as Suit could take it to the men. He made sure he doubled each drink and tripled the mounting bill the stripper would have to pay. Madame Woo, sitting on her perch with a fresh cigarette in her ivory holder was very pleased. A smile crept across her lined face as she watched how the men drank to the striptease taking place in the middle of the bar.

Bull and Sarge stood near the stripper, just in case he needed encouragement, and the hardhat was glad to entertain the men with his act rather than his ass. O'Reilly and Wolfe were busy untying the rookies. Their limbs sore from the tight bind of the knots, flushed with fresh blood going into them. They were very grateful to the two older cops and knelt before them, kissing their boots with their asses in the air.

The stripper now had his jeans down. He kicked one leg and the pant leg came off. Then he bent over, giving the crowd another look at his muscled ass before he bent down and picked up the pant leg and removed the other one. He now had only his hardhat on and the sweaty jock. With his pants removed, he used them to tease the crowd, pulling them through his legs, see-sawing back and forth the fabric in his ass-crack and rubbing his jock on the jeans.

The crowd was clapping to the beat. They howled and wanted more. The hardhat swung the jeans over his head in a circle as he slowly turned so the crowd could see every part of his body. The wide back, narrow hips, the line of hair that went down his chest and into the jock pouch, made him look mighty sexy and the crowd was eating it up.

The stripper flung the pants in the air and watched the crowd rip at them. He pulled on his jock, making his cock spring out, dripping hard. He turned and pulled on the straps so they slid into the crack of his ass. Then he bent way over and spread his cheeks, giving the crowd a good view of his virgin pucker by pulling on the straps until his hole spread open.

The crowd was throwing coins trying to hit his butt-hole. They went wild, taking out their cocks and waving them to the stripper.

Sarge barked at the hardhat, "Okay cocksucker. Pick up those quarters with your ass."

The stripper looked around the top of the table. There were quite a few quarters and some silver dollars. He decided to try the silver dollars first.

With the music pounding out a good beat, the hardhat wiggled his ass and squatted. His jock still on but the straps now in their proper place, he bent, squatted further down until he could feel the table on his butt cheeks. Not sure what to do he sat on the dollar and tried to squish it into his ass cheeks. It didn't work.

"Get to work whore, and pick up the money." Bull yelled.

The hardhat stood and shook his limbs. He got back into the rhythm and started his decent again. As he squatted and wiggled his ass he spread his legs wide and with the help of his hands, spread his cheeks and squatted on the silver dollar. Then he let go of his ass cheeks and stood. There in the crack of his butt was the shiny silver dollar. The crowd screamed with delight.

Men in the crowd began to pull up chairs and get their dicks out. They yelled at the hardhat. "Get the money pig. Come on, get more money little piggy."

The stripper loved it and placed the silver dollar in his jock. His smile matched the crack of his ass as he bent to retrieve a quarter. This time it worked even better. He was learning how to make his butt cheeks work."

"Fuck yeah." "Get it piggy. Get it for daddy." They yelled.

Now the hardhat was really getting into it. He waved his ass at the crowd. Bent over, spread his cheeks and had his sphincter wink for the men.

They went wild, jacking on their dicks, screaming to the stripper for more as they tossed every coin in their pockets along with bills.

The paper was easy and with each coin or bill, the jock weighed down and made his dick even harder. The mesh strained with its load and stretched obscenely and swayed to the beat playing on the jukebox.

"Sailor Boy!" called out Sarge.

"Sir. Yes Sir."

"Get your cap sailor and get over here. Now."

Tim grabbed his white navy hat and put it on his naked body. He presented himself to Sarge.

"This is for you sailor, you earned it. Put your cap out so that whore dancing up there can unload your booty."

"Hey slut!" yelled Sarge.

The hardhat walked over to Sarge, his jock hanging down with the weight of the money.

"Unload your take, mother-fucker and go back for more," Sarge barked.

Tim took his hat off. Standing there buck naked he held his cap up to the strained jock. The hardhat slowly peeled the top of his jock and watched the money flow out like a stream into the waiting cap. Tim then ran to where Madame Woo sat and dumped the catch on the bar top.

Madame Woo eyed the pile of silver and green and estimated her take. Tim went back for another fill. The cap took two loads of jock cash before it was empty. With a smile, Tim went back to bartend the thirsty crowd.

The hardhat was picking up nickels, dimes, even pennies. He picked up lighters and cigars. His ass squatted to take a finger or beer bottle. Men held up all kinds of things for the slut to grab with his pucker. He was getting tired too. It wasn't so much fun now when he bent and squatted for a penny. His butt-lips were sore from all the coinage, bottles, cigar butts and shot glasses he grabbed with his sphincter and wiggled to the crowd's glee.

Sarge had him pick up ashtrays with his ass and empty them. He had him sit on a broom stick and sweep the floor. The hardhat was sweating now. He dutifully did what Sarge wanted. Each task became more humiliating than the last.

Bull used the hardhat's jock for a leash. He led him around like a dog to squat on whatever was on the floor and pick it up. His butt was sore and he felt the fool but kept at it lest he anger Bull or Sarge.

With the floor cleaned and swept with the use of his ass, the men were getting horny watching the talented hole at work.

"How about a little man-pussy, Sarge?" someone asked.

The hardhat almost looked relieved when Sarge told him he was going to fuck, until he told him how.

"I want you to fuck yourself on every cock in the place. You do the work until they shoot or I'll use that dick of yours to catch sharks."

"Come here baby, daddy's got a pony for you to ride." A man said waving his barracuda.

Under the yellow hat streamed sweat that ran down his face. His back glistened with the work, marking the muscles in his shoulders tanned from the sun. He walked over and backed up to the man sitting on a chair with his cock in hand.

The hardhat spiked his ass on the heavy, big cock. He wiggled his ass to get it all in his butt.

"That's some talented ass you got there bitch." The man said and whacked the helmet on the construction workers head.

The bitch loved it. After picking up dimes, and everything else with his man-pussy, taking a big cock was easy; he thought, and proceeded to fuck himself on the prick.

"Work it baby. Work it for daddy," The man crooned to the hardhat that screwed himself on the man's cock.

"What that cunt needs is another prick up it," Sarge said and then instructed someone near to straddle the man in the chair and shove his cock in with the other.

The hardhat clenched his teeth fighting a wail deep in his guts. He had to push hard to fuck the two dicks planted in his ass and Sarge took his belt to the man's back to encourage him to fuck himself.

Sarge asked no one in particular, "Ya know what else this whore needs?"

"What Sarge," someone asked.

"He needs another cock in him. That's what this fucking slut needs. Who's gonna fuck his nasty face?"

Men scrambled to be the first to shove their dripping cock in the hardhat's face. One big guy pushed his way to the front and shoved a mean looking dick into the hardhat's mouth. The cocksucker's jaws were stretched to accommodate the big, thick, dick. His lips, stretched tight around the shaft, the hardhat could only gurgle in his agony.

The big guy had a smile on him and grabbed the cocksucker's helmet, using it to slam his prick in and out of the man's face. He slapped the construction guy. First one side and then the other until his cock glided in and out the man's throat.

"That's some good head. Damn good throat. Fuck it like pussy. Fuck it good," the big guy said and then spat on the cocksucker's face.

The hardhat's arms were flaying about. His butt, stuffed with two large cocks and his mouth pounded by a big dick made his eyes bug out, snot drained from his nose, he looked around, bewildered in his fight for a gasp of air. He didn't get any. The big guy pulled his club out and smashed the hardhat in the face with his fat prick, cock-slapping him. Before he could gasp enough air, the prick was shoved back in to the hilt.

CHAPTER TEN

Madame Woo was counting her take of the dance money when she heard a siren at the end of the pier. For most people, the shrill tone would have them look for the fire, but for Woo, it was the sound of money.

Six large firemen burst in the door of the bar with axes in hand. "Where's the fire Madame?" the captain asked.

"Right over there boys," she said pointing to the melee taking place around the hardhat.

Tim followed the six firemen that came in through the beaded curtain. His prick sticking up and his mouth dripping saliva, he tapped a dark haired fireman on the shoulder.

"I'm a firefighter on board ship. Can I help?" Tim said and with his last word, checked out the hot body he faced.

There was no shirt on the dark haired man. He wore suspenders to hold up his loose fitting, yellow fire pants. His helmet pushed back to let the dark curls on his forehead spring out. His cleft chin was as deep as the ridges in his tight, muscled abs. A big hard ass bounced in the loose pants and Tim noticed how white his butt-cheeks were compared to the tan of his torso.

The fireman gave the sailor a once over and smiled. "Sure ya can help buddy. How about taking a hold of this hose for me?" He then pulled out a big fat dick and waved it at Tim. The sailor grabbed it, but his hands couldn't get around the width. He fell to his knees and began to lather the head with his tongue.

"That's it fireman. You seem to handle a hose mighty fine."

Tim felt a large, gentle hand on the back of his head, guiding him to take more of the fireman's cock.

"That's it boy, take that fuckin dick. Take it cocksucker."

Another fireman looked at Tim's fine, hairless, bubble-butt sticking up in the air. Its little pink hole winked at him. The fireman dropped his axe and pulled out a foot long dick, he raised the ass just a bit and slammed his salami home.

"Fine piece of ass on this sailor, finest ass I've had in a long time," he said pumping in and out."

The other firefighters joined the gang fucking the hardhat. As soon as one guy came in his ass, another took over. Two cocks pumped the butt and one in his mouth. His limp body just took whatever prick came his way. He left his mouth opened to be mounted at anytime. His ass-hole stretched wide from two cocks fucking it constantly.

Bull was back tending bar. Madame Woo had slipped her loot into one of the pockets in her sleeve and lit incense to the ancestors for such good fortune. She then pulled out her ivory cigarette holder and fastened an Egyptian cigarette at its end.

The Chinese red silk lanterns cast a warm glow on the men. Their sweat glistened on their broad backs. Their narrow hips pumped back and forth, shoved hot cock meat deep in man-pussy and cock-sucking mouths. Suit was on the floor, licking shoes, sucking ass, taking dick. His hair was spotted with dried bits of cum. His body reeked of piss and he had dried spit on his back and a cock that stayed boned, drooling cock-snot.

The men used the furniture to throw others on their back to fuck them. They used the chairs to stand on for their hard round ass to be licked clean. They reclined in the sturdy, oak chairs for blowjobs. Men shoved their fingers and tongues in each other, making the butt-holes wet and juicy for good fucks. Some knelt to drink piss or suck cock, or both.

"Yeah, Sailor Boy, you take that fuckin' dick. Take it for Sarge." The drill instructor cooed in the ear of Tim.

He could see the sailor was getting into the reaming in his ass. Tim's lips, glued around a big dick in his mouth, sucked it all the way to the root.

Bull caught a glimpse of dawn coming up over the sea from a porthole window in the bar. The first hint of light hit the morning fog and turned in smoky gray. Men started to find boots and jocks, shirts and pants and slowly pulled them on. Whiskered, hung-over, they started to file out unto the damp wood wharf that held Madame Woo's bar.

As dawn's light crept through the cracks of Madam Woo's saloon, Sarge took Tim in his arms. He held him for a while as the sailor's ass-lips burped semen and his mouth dripped cum. Bull had Suit on clean-up duty. The bar slave was doing his best to lick up all the mess that oversexed men left behind on the floor, chairs and tables. Suit had yet to clean the head and stock the bar

Sarge sat in a chair and tenderly took the tips of his fingers and wiped the jizz from Tim's cheeks and lips. He then put his fingers in Tim's mouth for the sailor to nurse on.

"You had a good time, Sailor Boy? You got all the cock you wanted?"

Tim cooed and burped, sucking on Sarge's fingers feeding him gobs of jizz left on his face and chest. "I sure did Sarge. I got myself all filled up with cock."

"That's a good boy. You'll get big and strong like Sarge, with all that protein."

When Tim was through cleaning Sarge's fingers, he reached up and pulled open the sergeants shirt to suck on one of the marine's nipples.

"That's it Sailor, you must be tired after all that."

Tim moaned and lapped at the nipple nuzzled in his mouth. Sarge rocked him a bit while the men began to file out. It was almost six in the morning and Sarge needed to get Tim back on ship. He reached down and grabbed the butt-plug on the floor, sticking it back up Tim's ass. "We don't want you leaking when you board ship."

Then Sarge dressed him tenderly, putting Tim's jock on and trying to stuff the sailor's stretched out balls and bloated cock back into the pouch before he put on the sailor's pants and shirt.

Sarge placed his arm around the sailor and headed for the door, the last to leave. He wanted to make sure Tim got on his ship and to say goodbye to him until sailor's next shore leave.

Madam Woo looked out the door as Sarge tenderly guided Tim down the wharf with his arm around the sailor's shoulder. The sea fog was in, blocking out the dawn. The winos and derelicts were lining up in back of the bar at the edge of the wharf with a quarter in each hand. Madam Woo figured Suit would have enough quarters that he could start taking it in the ass the next day.

She turned, and before climbing the stairs said, "Good night Bull, put Suit out before you turn off lights. He has cash customers lined up."

"Will do Madam Woo, sleep tight and don't let the bed bugs bite."

"They leave me alone. I bite back," she chuckled as she walked up the stairs.

ABOUT THE AUTHOR

Michael V. Gleich is a writer that has no one genre. His work includes erotica, mysteries, romance, horror and comedy. When not writing his latest short story, he works on novels. His short works have been published by the Harrington Gay Men's Literary Quarterly and appeared on websites such as Sexy Sayer  and Nifty.org. Michael has also published numerous non-fiction articles for several different websites including Page Wise and Fine Tuning. His articles reflect his expertise in travel, bicycling and surfing. He is a long time member of Writer's Village University, where he continues to hone his craft.